ALL OUR PRETTY SONGS

ALL OUR PRETTY SONGS

SARAH McCARRY

ST. MARTIN'S GRIFFIN ⚞ NEW YORK

ALL OUR PRETTY SONGS. Copyright © 2013 by Sarah McCarry. All rights reserved. Printed in the United States of America. For information, address St. Martin's Press, 175 Fifth Avenue, New York, N.Y. 10010.

www.stmartins.com

Design by Anna Gorovoy

Dirty Wings excerpt copyright © 2013 by Sarah McCarry.

The Library of Congress Cataloging-in-Publication Data
is available upon request

ISBN 978-1-250-04088-6 (hardcover)
ISBN 978-1-250-02708-5 (trade paperback)
ISBN 978-1-250-02709-2 (e-book)

First Edition: August 2013

10 9 8 7 6 5 4 3 2 1

What, then, could she complain of,
except that she had been loved?

—OVID

At least I have the flowers of myself,
and my thoughts, no god
can take that

—H.D.

JULY

Aurora and I live in a world without fathers. Hers is dead and mine was gone before I was born. Her house in the hills is full of his absence: his guitars in every room, his picture on all the walls, his flannel shirts and worn-through jeans still hanging in the closets, his platinum records on the mantel of the marble fireplace that is so big we both used to crawl inside it when we were little. He is everywhere, and so we never think about him. Aurora's mother is a junkie and mine is a witch. When I say it like that, it sounds funny, but that doesn't mean it's not true.

This is a story about love, but not the kind of love you think. You'll see.

Aurora and I grew up like sisters, and this is how we match: same bony, long-toed feet; same sharp elbows; same single crooked tooth (Aurora's left canine, my right front). Same way of looking at you out of the corners of our eyes until you blush. Same taste in music: faster, harder, more. Same appetite. Same heart.

Aurora and I live like sisters, but we are not alike. I am tidy, and Aurora has never cleaned a mess she made in her life. Aurora sleeps until four if you let her, loves *Aliens*, smiles often, is the kind of girl who will break into your car to leave you a present you don't know you want until you find it. Aurora's mom is richer than anything you can imagine, and mine is poor. Aurora is sunlight, and I'm a walking scowl. Aurora's skin is dark, and mine is watery cream. She bleaches her black hair white and smokes unfiltered Lucky Strikes and drinks too much. She wears dresses made out of white lace and gloves with the fingers cut off, Converse with holes at the toes and old-lady satin pumps, and if you think right now of the most beautiful girl you know, Aurora next to that girl is a galaxy dwarfing an ordinary sun.

I am not beautiful at all, but I am mean. Every day I wear black jeans and the worn-out Misfits shirt that used to be Aurora's dad's and combat boots with steel in the toes. People keep away from my fists in the pit at shows. I cut my dark hair short and my eyes are grey like smoke when I am happy and like concrete when I am not. Every morning I get up at six and run seven miles, into the hills and back, and where Aurora's body is model-skinny, mine is solid muscle sheathed in a soft layer that all the miles in the world can't skim away. Aurora breaks hearts, and I paint pictures. We are both pretty good at what we do.

Before we were born our moms lived like sisters, too. They drove up and down the coast in Maia's diesel Mercedes, following punk bands and sleeping on the beach, dyeing each other's hair pink and blue and orange and green. Maia met Aurora's dad backstage at a show in Los Angeles, before anyone knew how famous he would be. Back then he was just a sad-eyed boy from a shitty town in the Northwest with a guitar and dirty clothes. Maia chased him out into the parking lot and they fell in love as the moon rose over the Pacific. Cass drove them around while they kissed in the backseat. "It was so much fun we drove to Mexico," Cass said, the only time she told me the story. The three of them spent a week living on the beach and swimming naked in the ocean every day, sleeping on striped blankets they bought in a market. They had no money, but that was a time when you didn't need money, when it was enough to be young and beautiful and in love. Cass drove them back to LA and they got married in a twenty-four-hour chapel next to the freeway, with Cass as their witness and a hungover Elvis impersonator officiating. Neither Cass nor Maia owned a dress. Maia wore a white slip she'd bought that afternoon in a thrift store and a headdress Cass made her out of roses and silk ribbons. Cass wore cutoffs, a dog collar, and the Misfits shirt she stole from Aurora's dad and later gave to me. Before the year was over Aurora's dad would make one of the bestselling albums of all time, and then Maia and Cass would have Aurora and me, and then everything would fall apart. Now Maia sleeps away the years like a friendless fairy-tale princess behind a wall of thorns, and Aurora's dad is dead, and Cass and I are stuck in the real world of never having enough money for bills despite all of Cass's spells.

"But that week," Cass said. "That week was the most perfect week of my life." Maybe it was perfect for Maia, too. I've never thought to ask.

Aurora's room is like an antique store and a record store exploded while mating. Posters hang all over the walls: Arthur Rackham prints, the Pixies, a wet cat hanging from a tree branch with the motto HANG IN THERE. Aurora's embellished the cat with a markered-on mustache and fedora. Piles of magazines, *Vogue* and *Ben is Dead* and *Spin*, *Sassy* with all the quizzes dog-eared and filled out in different-colored inks (red for Aurora's answers, blue for mine). Every inch of wall that isn't covered in posters is covered in pictures: Aurora in her dad's arms as a baby, his face already haunted; Aurora and me at every stage of development, from infants with the same fat, formless faces to our first junior-high dance (Aurora in sunglasses to hide how stoned she is, me looking serious and faintly alarmed); Aurora and Maia; Cass and Maia. The famous picture from *Rolling Stone*: Aurora as a wide-eyed toddler, clutching her father's guitar, surrounded by the members of his band. It was taken right after he died. The guitar dwarfs her. It's an original print, unframed, tacked carelessly next to a sheaf of dried roses tied together with a dirty ribbon and hanging from a nail. Empty Dr Pepper cans and sticks of incense, rhinestone-covered dresses, Christmas lights and piles of silk scarves, an empty bottle of Chanel No. 5 in a dish full of quarters. Her dad's record collection—crate after crate of old punk and new wave, obscure soul music, seven-inches his band recorded before they were famous. Books on witchcraft, travel guides, old anatomical textbooks, *Flowers in the Attic*. Her battered copy of *Tam Lin* that we traded back and forth as kids until the covers fell off. *Winterlong* and *Weetzie Bat*.

I used to borrow Aurora's clothes, but as I got older, as it became apparent I'd be the draft ox to her dragonfly, I quit shimmer for death-metal gloom. But sometimes when we're bored we stay up all night eating ice cream and listening to her dad's records. We raid Aurora's makeup drawer for mascara wands and compacts of pressed powder; iridescent eyeshadows; rich, dark-red lipsticks by the handful. I let her paint my eyelids with the intense concentration of an old master, color my lips a Jazz Age maroon. We take Polaroids of ourselves and tape them to her walls, steal Maia's video camera and film ourselves gyrating to the Clash. When we're finally exhausted we fall asleep in her giant bed, curled around each other in a pile of silk and feathers. We don't wake up until long after the morning sun gives way to afternoon.

Tonight, we're catnapping in Aurora's bed, watching *Heathers* for the fortieth time and eating Cheetos. Cass would die a thousand agonized deaths if she saw the color of the chemicals going into my mouth. Aurora's in love with Christian Slater, but I think he is too cheesy, even as JD. It's a longstanding bone of contention between us. "Look at him." I lick fluorescent orange powder off my fingertips. "He's, like, engineered in a factory. A factory for teenage girls."

"You comprehend nothing," Aurora says, wounded. "I would totally have gone the distance. Winona Ryder isn't worthy."

"He tries to kill her," I point out.

"Only because she wouldn't follow through with her own vision. You have to commit. That's the lesson. God, look at those *cheekbones*." But nothing she says can convince me. There's no real torment behind those eyes. JD is a sham.

"How very." I smirk. Aurora hits me with a pillow.

When the movie is over it's time to go out. Aurora puts on Joy Division and turns it all the way up, knots her bleach-white hair, paints her mouth vampire-purple, puts on dresses and takes them off again, dancing around the room in her underwear. I pretend to be bored. It's our ritual. When she's ready we drive downtown in the old Mercedes that used to be Maia's, windows down, the Jesus and Mary Chain cranked so loud we can't hear ourselves talk. We have fake IDs, but we rarely need them. I've never seen anyone say no to Aurora. We're barely inside the club before someone's buying her one drink, and then another, boys and girls getting in line to cajole her into a smile. Every other drink she hands to me, but I give them back most of the time. Somebody has to keep us safe on the way home. Aurora never thinks about what comes after; she's all now, all the time. This moment, this kiss, this second holds everything. People like Aurora don't have to live with consequences. The stage lights go down and we push our way to the front, ready for magic, for wild rumpus, for anything. Ready to go ecstatic.

Tonight, we aren't disappointed. This band is on fire. The singer's tiny, her shaggy red-dyed hair sticking up like a ragged halo. She's wearing a long-sleeved thermal, its fraying sleeves hanging to her knuckles, her bony fingers barely visible against the guitar strings. The music is heavy, a sludgy mass of guitar that makes the room seem even darker. When she opens her mouth to sing the voice that rips out of her is a banshee howl climbing to an operatic shriek. She paces the stage in smaller and smaller circles, pivoting around the axis of the mic stand, energy crackling off her in waves, never once looking at the audience. The drummer is moving so fast her arms are blurs. The bassist plays the way I love best, cigarette dangling, eyes closed, completely still except for his fingers. Like he's asleep standing up, too cool even to acknowledge how good he is.

Here's me and Aurora in the pit: hot press of bodies, humid smoke-thick air, the two of us up against the stage, elbows planted on the dirty wood. When the music starts with a roar we throw ourselves backward into the crush of people behind us. All the way inside our bodies and all the way outside them at the same time. A wall of noise crashes through us, washing us clean. Like when we are on the edge of coming and the whole world blows wide open for a second and we can see all the way to the center where everything is still. Guitar so loud we can feel it in our chests. Someone else's hair in our faces and someone else's knuckles in our teeth and sometimes, when it's really good, a current charges from body to body and everyone around us is part of it, part of us, part of the drumbeat thundering through us so hard our breathing shifts to follow its pulse. Music turns us inside out with hunger, the need to hurt ourselves, get drunk, fuck, punch strangers, the need to take off all our clothes and run around in the grass screaming, the need get in a car and drive off in the middle of the night with a pack of strangers. We let the music shake us loose from the moorings of our bodies and hearts and brains, until we are nothing but sex and sweat and fists and hot hot light.

Up front we are often the only girls, and we learned early to make a space for ourselves, to punch if anyone gets too close in the wrong way, kick out like boys, throw ourselves at everyone around us like our bodies are stones. People know who we are now, know Aurora's face and my fists, smile at us, leave room. Sometimes a boy will kneel down, weave both hands into a step for one of us, let us put one booted foot into the cradle of his fingers and then catapult us over the crowd, hands rising to keep us aloft, carrying us to the edge of the stage and then back again. Our bodies are rafts moving across a sea of brothers, fathers, lovers. The air is charged and reckless. Up front is when I feel all the way alive, deep in my animal body, a live wire humming electric. Me and Aurora together, like sisters, like twins. Do you know what it's like to be a girl pieced together out of appetite and impulse? We do. In that place of heat and noise I forget everything, forget being poor and being scared, forget the looming misery of school and the adult world, forget walls and masks and pretense. Up front I forget everything except drum and guitar and heat, the anchor of Aurora's hand in mine as we're tossed across an ocean made out of bodies, breathless and alive and blooming with sound.

When the show is over we are soaked and panting, holding each other tight. Aurora's eyes are huge. "Oh my god. That was, like, the best." The boy standing next to us is already trying to ask her name, but she ignores him. "Come backstage," she says to me. "I know that girl."

This is the part I hate. I like to keep the magic close, not ruin it with people. "I kind of want to go home."

"Are you kidding? You're no *fun*."

I sigh. "Okay." She takes my hand and tows me after the band. Backstage, she hops in place while they drag their amps offstage, take apart the drum kit and cart it to their van. I stand, awkward, digging the toe of my boot into the concrete floor. The singer comes over to us and gives Aurora a hug. Up close she's even more beautiful than she was on stage. I'm so shy I don't know where to look. She and Aurora jump straight into gossip. The bass player, still cool, lurks nearby, pretending not to pay attention.

"You got a light?" It's the drummer.

"Yeah, sure." I follow her outside. Behind the club the alleyway is dark. I light her cigarette for her, and then mine. "You guys were great."

"Thanks." She smokes like she wants to chew on the filter, taps her fingers against her thighs. She's wearing a white men's undershirt. The muscles in her arms ripple as she brings the cigarette to her mouth, patters out a rhythm with her free hand. "You know Aurora?"

"Yeah. She's like my sister."

"Same mom? You don't look alike."

"No, grew up together."

"Yeah?"

"We lived in the same house for a long time. Our moms are old friends." This is not exactly the truth. Our moms *were* old friends. Our moms haven't spoken since I was a kid.

"You knew her dad?"

"I mean, kind of. I don't remember him. We were really young when he died."

"Fucked up."

"Yeah." I wait for her to pry. I'm used to deflecting questions about Aurora, about her dad, about her life, about her money. But she drops it.

"Sorry. That's messed up to ask. I can never think of the right thing to say to people."

I laugh. "Me, either. Aurora's the one who's good at that stuff. I stand around."

"You play?"

"Me? No."

"She doesn't either, right?"

"No."

"I guess that's some pretty heavy stuff to carry around. Shit," she says, exhaling. "There I go again. Sorry."

"No, it's okay."

We smoke the rest of our cigarettes in silence. Back inside, the bass player's made his move, slinking up to Aurora as she chirps away. The euphoria of the show has worn off. My ears are ringing and I'm tired. I can tell by the way Aurora is leaning into the bass player that it's going to be a long night.

The band invites us over. I make Aurora let me drive, follow their beat-up van to an old industrial neighborhood down by the water. Their apartment is the whole third floor of an abandoned factory. It's obviously supposed to be a practice space, but they have a hot plate plugged into a wall and a curtained-off toilet that I guess passes as a bathroom. Every surface is covered with overflowing ashtrays, coffee mugs stuffed with cigarette butts, empty beer cans, half-empty bottles of whisky. There are nests of blankets and clothes in three corners of the enormous room. Somebody, more ambitious than the rest of the band, has gone so far as to hang a moldy shower curtain from the ceiling for privacy. I walk over to the huge windows that overlook the bay and try to ignore the smell. This place must be freezing in the winter, but underneath the filth it's pretty amazing. I can see the streaming lights of cars on the viaduct, and past that the wine-dark water. Far away, the firefly glow of a ferry moves toward the far horizon.

"Pretty great view, huh?" It's the drummer again. Behind me the bassist is pouring Aurora a drink. I can hear him apologize for the lack of ice, and she giggles.

"Yeah. I want a place like this someday."

"What would you do with all this space?"

"I paint." I try to say it naturally, but it sounds funny. *I'm a painter.* Maybe in my dreams. Lah-dee-dah.

"Yeah? That's cool. I can't even draw stick figures. All I'm good at is drumming and washing dishes."

"People were really into you."

"There's a million bands in this city, and at least ten of them are good. Not enough to go around. I might still be washing dishes when I'm thirty."

"At least you tried."

"Not many other options." I nod. We're quiet again. She takes out another cigarette, smokes it, taps. I wonder if she twitches in her sleep. She's waiting for me. We are entering the realm of adult transactions. But I don't want to sleep here, and so I don't say anything. I bring my shoulders up to my ears and make the silence hard and without invitation. I hear Aurora's laugh again, and the noise of more people coming into the loft. Someone puts on an old punk record, something loud and fast that I don't recognize. A shot of nervousness runs through me and I chew on my lip, curl my toes in my boots. The drummer leaves me at the window. I don't want to turn around, deal with strangers. I want to grab Aurora and get out of here. I turn enough to see what she's up to. Kissing the bass player on the couch while people sit on the other end, ignoring them, drinking beer and handing around records. Oh, Aurora. For a young dog, her tricks are pretty old.

I wait until Aurora comes up for air and then I sidle over. "I'm out." The bassist's a skeeze, but he's pretty tame compared to some of the dudes Aurora ends up with. These people seem nice. They'll take care of her if anything goes wrong. Hold her hair out of her face while she throws up their shitty whisky. I'm far from home, but not too far to walk. She looks up at me.

"Take my car."

"No, it's fine. I'll walk."

"I don't want you to walk."

"I like walking."

"Serious." She rummages through her purse, looking for her keys. I dig them out of my pocket and try to give them to her, but she closes my fingers around them. "Serious," she says again. "I'll get a ride home with—" She stops, turns to the bass player. "What's your name again?" For a second, he looks hurt, and then his face is cool again. She'll eat him for breakfast, I think, and I can't help grinning. She knows why I'm smiling, and she throws her head back and laughs. "I'll be fine, Mom."

"Okay."

"I love you."

"I love you, too."

To my surprise, Cass is waiting up for me. She takes a bowl of stir-fry out of the refrigerator. "I can heat it up," she offers. I shake my head, sit at the table, and shove forkfuls of vegetables and tofu into my mouth. Cass has been a health freak for about as long as I've been sentient. She quit doing drugs when I was a kid. Unfortunately for me, she also quit sugar, television, and fun. She insists the human body is meant to live on raw food, but I told her I'd run away from home if she got rid of the stove, so we compromise. She makes me stir-fry and herbal tea, and I don't tell her when I go to Chinatown with Aurora and eat sixteen different kinds of meat swimming in grease. That way, everybody's happy. Mostly. I would give anything to have a secret stash of, say, pork rinds, but Cass can sniff out Yellow #5 the way some moms suss pot and dirty thoughts. She was nineteen when she had me, and most of the time she feels like an annoying friend you can't shake and not like a mom at all. But when it comes to restricting my toxin intake, she's a holy terror.

"You out with Aurora?"

"Yeah."

"Good show?"

"Yeah, they were awesome. We hung out with them for a while. She's still there. Not really my scene, though." Cass snags a red pepper out of my bowl.

"You worried about her?"

"Like, all the time. But not tonight."

"Okay." Her face goes distant and I know she's thinking of Maia. Aurora would be better off in the custody of a potato. At least she could eat it if things got dire. "You let me know, though, if—" She trails off. *If what?* I want to ask. *If Aurora gets loaded every weekend and goes home with boys who are basically strangers?* Kind of late in the game for team D.A.R.E.

"It's cool. She's cool. I keep an eye on her."

"That's my girl." Cass reaches over to ruffle my hair, and I duck. I hate it when she tries to be a parent. It doesn't suit her.

Lately I have been dreaming about a river and a dark forest. In the dream I am standing on a path that winds through trees that are white as bone and without leaves. I am barefoot, and my feet are covered in blood. The only light comes from the trees themselves, an opaline glow like that of a luminescent fungus. The path stops at a river that is too broad for me to see the far bank, and the water moves swift and smooth and has an oily sheen to it. I know there is someone waiting for me on the other side, someone I must find, but I do not know who it is. In the distance I can hear howling. Wolves, I think, or dogs. The bare branches of the trees clatter against one another although there is no wind. I take a step forward, but before my foot breaks the surface of the water I wake up. It is always a long time before I remember where I am.

———

After Aurora's father died, when I was still very small, Cass and I lived with Aurora and Maia for a while. The house was always full of people and music then. Maia was a silent shadow, worn wraithlike with grief. She moved further and further away from us, into her own twilit limbo outside space and time. Sometimes a skeleton-thin man in a long black coat would come to the house and sit in her room with her for hours. Cass told us he was her doctor, but we didn't know then the kind of medicine he was working with his suitcase full of needles and glassine bags. Aurora and I weren't allowed in Maia's part of the house, but we stole into it once. I remember candles everywhere, and dark walls without decoration, and a great canopied bed draped with silk and satin and scattered with velvet pillows. Maia slept tangled in the sheets, her arms akimbo, her mouth slack, her nut-brown skin ashen. "Is she dead?" I whispered.

"She's fine," Aurora said. "She sleeps a lot."

Slowly Aurora's father's bandmates and their friends drifted away, escaping their orbit around the black hole Maia had become. There were no more parties, where Aurora and I darted in between the legs of grown-ups, stole bites off plates and sips out of glasses and fell asleep, giddy and a little drunk, on Aurora's lawn. No more circles of musicians playing guitars together in the garden until the sky glowed white with dawn. No more lanky-limbed, long-haired men and women twirling us around while we squealed with glee, lifting us to their shoulders and parading us up and down the sweeping marble staircase, or teaching us to slide down the banisters when Cass wasn't paying attention. The house went still and dead as a tomb.

After that, Cass took me away from Aurora's palace in the hills. Aurora and I stayed twin-blooded, wearing each other's clothes and finishing each other's sentences, but Cass and Maia never talked again. I don't know what happened in that vast house, or if anything happened at all. Maybe Cass gave up trying to pull Maia out of darkness and settled for bringing me to a brighter world instead. Sometimes I wish Cass had fought harder, had taken Aurora and Maia with us. I know it was hard for Cass to get clean, and maybe that's why she left Maia there; she wasn't strong enough for them both. I'm not like that. I will never let go of anything I love.

Aurora and I have lived in this city all our lives. If you came here you would know that it is a young city, out on the edge of the world, just a few hours away from where the earth drops off into the grey ocean that reaches all the way to the far edge of the sky. It is a city of hills and water, ringed in mountains that are capped with white even in the dead of July. The summers are sweet and golden, bookended with long rainy seasons where the sky brushes the earth with a blanket of cloud.

Aurora and I used to spend our days roaming, picking out books at the huge old bookstore downtown with its creaking wooden floors and innumerable rooms, trying on Doc Martens and buying Manic Panic at the punk store under the viaduct, stuffing ourselves with fish and chips on the pier and drinking coffee until our speedy hands shook. We haunted the curio store down on the waterfront, visiting Sylvia and Sylvester, its glass-cased mummies (Aurora insists they are real; I say no way). Even now we still love putting quarters in the fortune-telling machine and watching the turban-swathed mannequin inside move its jerky mechanical hand and spit out fortunes printed on cardboard squares. Aurora always gets the good ones. On the curiosity-laden shelves a fetal pig bobs in a bath of formaldehyde next to a stuffed two-headed lamb. The store manager once let me take Aurora's picture with the lamb.

We love best the coffee shop up on the hill, a veritable stable of goths and artists. Tall, many-paned windows let in the light, and the red-painted walls are lined with bookshelves. When we were kids Aurora and I would bum cigarettes off cute boys playing guitar at the outdoor tables. She'd pen tortured poetics in her journal while I surreptitiously tried to draw everyone around us. The baristas with their multicolored hair and deliberately ragged clothes, most of them stained with paint or some other indicator of artistic temperament. The strung-out rockers, blinking into their coffee. The street kids hitting us up for quarters and trying to get Aurora's phone number.

It was easy to pretend I was an adult in those moments: the rain-dampened streets outside the window, the air hazy with cigarette smoke, the whir of the espresso machine, the low murmur of people talking around us. An adult with a bookstore job, maybe, and a musician boyfriend who would write songs about me. We would stay up all night smoking pot and having sex, and we would only allow our apartment to be illuminated by candlelight. Every room would be hung with glittering beaded curtains. Cass had no tolerance for my preadolescent passions; when I brought home a stack of Jane's Addiction records she scoffed. "Smacked-out posers," she said disdainfully. I couldn't explain to her that there was something in that wash of noise that felt like home to me. Cass and Maia had lived for punk shows when they were our age, but Cass never even went out anymore. Never went with us to the dirty all-ages clubs we spent our weekends in, or the bars we started frequenting as soon as Aurora was old and charming enough to get us past the door. Cass still had all her old records, but I never heard her play them. Finally, one day a few years ago, I dragged them all into my room and kept them there.

When Aurora and I were kids Cass would take us hiking in the woods outside the city. We'd pick our way across the loamy forest floor, our noses flooded with the green dark smell of moss, of mushrooms coming up out of the damp earth, of fallen trees crumbling into soil and new trees springing up out of the old, their roots snaking through the dead, rain-slick trunks. We'd climb narrow rocky paths up out of the woods, clinging to the sides of mountains, picking our way through alpine meadows awash in monkshood, lupine, and scarlet paintbrush. I loved the immense, vivid silence up there, the way a single marmot cry would echo and echo through the far hills. Up there you felt like you were all alone on the roof of the world, nothing but razor-edged ridges and high peaks as far as you could see in all directions.

These days Aurora isn't interested in wild places, and Cass rarely has time anymore. As soon as I learned how to drive I started borrowing Cass's car and going out on my own. I spend the morning panting my way up switchbacks so steep I think sometimes I'll tip over backward. Later, I'll drive home through broken-down logging towns with trailer parks full of moldering doublewides, where men lean against the bar in the one restaurant in town even though it's only three or four in the afternoon. I'll order hamburgers, or milkshakes, fried eggs and sausage, the kinds of foods Cass never allows across the threshold of our house, and pick at the greasy mess on my plate, wondering how my life would be different if one of those men was my father. Sometimes I see kids my own age. They stare me down, mean-eyed, and I always look away first.

You learn a lot about yourself when you spend most of your time alone. If I'm not with Aurora, I'm never with anyone. Aurora is happiest as the sun at the center of a solar system, and I'm at peace as a quiet moon, no light coming from me but the light that was hers first.

It's hard if you are a girl like Aurora, easier if you are a girl like me. I'm not the one old gods hanker after, not the one likely to be invited to immortals' parties. The Fates don't bother with small fry like me. I was never jealous of Aurora, not of her beauty or her money or her sad fairy-tale life. I loved her with every corner of my dark and crooked heart. People said our names together in a single breath, like we were two halves of the same body, like they could not imagine either one of us on our own.

I was never jealous, I should say, until him.

I'm smoking a cigarette and trying to draw the ocean when Aurora calls. "How weary, stale, flat, and unprofitable all the uses of the world are seeming. Right? Are you with me?" I make a noncommittal noise. "Exactly. I'm going to have a party. Come over." I know better than to argue, promise I'll be there in an hour. I grab my bag and unlock my bike from where it's chained to a pipe in the alley behind our apartment building. The night feels dangerous and too warm. It's the kind of dark that makes you reckless, sends an itch creeping under your skin. This summer is the hottest I can remember. The air smells like jasmine and, underneath, the sea. The moon is low and huge in the sky.

I'm tired by the time I've bicycled the long miles to Aurora's house, and I stand for a while in the shadows of her garden, catching my breath. When Aurora was younger there was an assortment of gardeners and assistants to keep up the grounds and take care of the house, but one by one they've straggled away over the years. These days, the house is lurching into a kind of derelict glamour. The once velvet-soft green lawn has been overtaken by wildflowers and straggling vines. Thorny hedges of blackberry have swallowed the wrought-iron fence that marks the edge of their property. The house itself is overrun with jasmine and St. John's wort; yellow and purple flowers wind up the columns of the front porch, obscuring most of the house, and battle for supremacy with the ivy that shrouds the chimneys and hangs in green tendrils across the windows. Aurora seems unconcerned about her house's slide into disrepair. "I like it," she says. "Maybe one day my mother will wake up and notice her entire life is falling apart around her, and then she can clean it up."

The first floor of her house is open and angular, and I can see through the plate-glass windows to the vaulted ceilings and vast white expanses, the huge abstract canvases that hang here and there: a savage red square on a yellow background, a field of blue, another field of white. Behind a slab of marble, a tattooed bartender in an old-fashioned suit pours drinks. In the yard, Aurora has hung paper lanterns in the trees. The roses are blooming. Her house is full of people. Industry people, ostentatiously uncool, making sure you know how much they don't care about anything except music. Stubble-cheeked boys in cutoff shorts over thermals, hair hanging to their shoulders, talking in big voices about their bands, their tours, their perennially breaking-down vans, telling the same old musician stories. Some of the women are in vacuumed-tight dresses, their mouths painted on in glossy red slashes. I have no idea who they're trying to impress. Any of these dudes will sleep with you for clean sheets and a free breakfast. No reason to even bother with brushing your hair.

I look for Maia. When she's more or less sober she likes to prance around, play the queen. She still has all her old party dresses, sequins and leather and lace, though too much speed and too many long nights have stripped the flesh off her bones until she's skeleton-gaunt, like those scary yoga ladies you see lurking in the aisles of health-food stores whispering about master cleanses and organ detox. Maia still has a faint echo of the glory of her youth, and when she's on she's like champagne: a bubbly thing that buoys you along, makes you feel special. I know Maia too well to be charmed by anything she does, but seeing her gussied up at parties is the green flash that shows up on your lids when you close your eyes after staring at the sun. Aurora's the real deal, but Maia can dazzle you if you're not used to the light.

I see her at last, leaning against a tree with a tumbler in one hand and a lit cigarette in the other. Her straight black hair looks dirty and there are circles under her eyes that accentuate the sharp line of her cheekbones. Not sober, then. "Hi, Maia," I say.

"Hi, sweetheart. Thanks for coming." She sucks on the cigarette like it's her last meal. *When* was *her last meal?* I wonder, eyeing the stark lines of her clavicle. "Aurora's having a good time," she says, pointing. Aurora's across the yard. Her bleached hair is piled on top of her head and she's wearing a sequined dress that grazes the tops of her long thighs. She hasn't seen me yet. Maia and I watch her flit from person to person, dipping in like a hummingbird taking sips. "She never talks to me anymore. All grown up now, you girls." This is not exactly fair; it is hard to talk to Maia, since half the time she is too high to know who either of us are.

"Mmm," I say. "She's busy."

"She have a boyfriend?"

"I don't think she's very interested in settling down."

"You girls." Her face is wistful. Junkies getting nostalgic. Cute. "You grow up so fast." She's repeating herself. We've had this conversation before. If I let her, we'll have it again before the night is out. You think I'm being unkind, and maybe I am, but I'm the one who's had to get Aurora out of strangers' houses, track her down when she disappears, sober her up enough to make it home, cover for her when she's too fucked up for school. Maia loves her, loves us both, but if she were running the show we'd probably both be dead.

"I should see if Aurora needs any help." I move my arm in a vague gesture that I hope conveys helpfulness.

"Of course, sweetie. Come back and talk to me later."

When Aurora sees me, she hugs me tight, and I smell her skin: vanilla and patchouli and cigarettes. She is already drunk. From the edge of her garden I can see the still-lit windows of the office buildings far below us, and past that the bay. The moon's reflection glimmers on the sound, a silver road on dark water. When we were little Aurora and I thought that path of light would take us to some distant, marvelous country. I assume this party will be like every other one of Aurora's parties, but that's where I'm wrong. This is the party where we meet Jack, and nothing will be the same again.

In the telling, I want to make up some sign, but the first time I see him is only ordinary. I know right away that he's beautiful, but there's no violin swelling, no chorus of stage-left witches spelling out our future when our eyes first meet. He's leaning on a crumbling stone wall. Long legs, torn jeans, a shirt worn thin enough that I can see the outline of his body through the fabric. His skin is darker than Aurora's and seems to catch and hold the light that drifts down from the lanterns. His hair snakes in coils to his shoulders. Dreadlocked, I think, but when I get closer I can see it's hundreds of braids. There's a guitar next to him. A cool breeze comes up behind me and hisses in my ear. A loose half-circle of people has formed around him, holding their drinks and gossiping idly. "Come on," Aurora says.

"Who's that?"

"We're going to find out."

We sidle between a couple of dudes in high tops and flannel, identical manes of long brown hair. The boy with the guitar touches the strings, and a hush falls across the garden. And then he begins to play.

A single note, faint and sweet, travels all the way from the stars to fall lightly to earth, and then another, scattering soft as rain. His music is like nothing I have ever heard. It is like the ocean surging, the wind that blows across the open water, the far call of gulls. It catches at my hair, moves across my skin and into my mouth and under my tongue. I can feel it running all through me. It is open space and mountains, the still-dark places of the woods where no human beings have walked for hundreds of years, loamy earth and curtains of green moss hanging from the ancient trees. Salmon swimming against the current, dying as they leave their eggs, birthing another generation to follow the river back to the sea. Red-gold blur of a deer bounding through the woods. Snowmelt in spring, bears lumbering awake as the rivers swell, my own body stirring as though all my life has been a long winter slumbered away and I'm only now coming into the day-lit world. As he plays the party stills. Birds flutter out of the trees to land at his feet and he is haloed in dragonflies and even the moonlight gathers around him as though the sky itself is listening. The music fills every place in my body, surges hot and bright in my chest. At last he stops. Aurora's mouth is open, her cheeks flushed. One of the flannel shirts is weeping openly. I can't catch my breath.

A stranger is standing beside me now, very still. He is tall and so thin he's just a rattle of bones wired together. He's dressed in elegant, close-cut black clothes and a long black coat despite the summer heat. He is staring at the guitar player with a fixed intensity; not the awe or sorrow marking the faces of everyone around us, but something that looks more like hunger.

"That was beautiful," I say to him, wanting to acknowledge somehow what we've witnessed even though the words feel worse than inadequate. He looks down at me and nods. For a moment I think there is red fire where his eyes should be, burning in the sockets of his cadaver's face, and I bring my hand to my mouth in shock; but he blinks, and then he is human again. I back away from him, into Aurora, and he smiles a smile with too many teeth. He looks past me, sees Aurora, and his eyes widen. That same hunger, but even more focused. He nods at me again, and then he turns away from me and walks back across the garden.

"Whoa," Aurora says. "Do you know that guy?"

"No," I say, shaken. Around me the party slowly comes to life again, people shaking themselves and blinking, dazed and forlorn. Aurora takes my hand and leads me closer to the guitar player. He puts the guitar away in a battered case, stands up, stretches, sees us.

"Hi," he says.

"Hi," Aurora says. "We're your future. I think you should tell us everything."

His name is Jack. He's come here from somewhere in the South, he won't say where, and he thinks the summers are nice here but the winters are too cold, and he's lived all over, and he plays for money wherever he goes. Sometimes the money is good. Most of the time it isn't. He's here to take his chances with the big leagues, like everyone else who got off a bus downtown in the last few years. He lives in a little house in town, washes dishes all day to pay the rent, plays every night until the stars begin their long fall into sunrise, does the whole thing again. Aurora is standing like a colt, one foot turned inward. She looks at him through the white curtain of her hair, which has come loose from its knot and hangs around her like a cloud. "Come away with us."

"Right now?" he asks. She nods. "Isn't this your party?"

"These people," she says, contemptuous. "They'll be fine."

Aurora's too drunk. "I'll drive," I say. She pouts, but she gives me the keys. We roll down all the windows in her car and let the night in. He sits in the back, leans his elbows on the headrests of our seats. His mouth is inches from my ear. I take us to the park Aurora and I loved best when we were children, rolling grassy hills at the very edge of the water, next to an abandoned factory surrounded by a chain-link fence. The buildings loom alien and strange in the moonlight. We walk to the place where the grass ends in a thin strip of sand at the edge of the water. Aurora collapses gracefully. I follow, less so. He lies between us in the grass. My skin hums electric, so close to his. Some key connection shorts out in my head and my brain goes dark, neatly wiped of reason. I want to roll over and take a bite out of his shoulder. Pummel him with my fists. I can hear the beat of his heart, I swear. The fabric of his shirt whispers as he breathes. All the cells in my body rearrange, compass needles pointing to his north. I could do anything, anything, anything, wonderful things, terrible things, all the things. Hit him, grab him, kiss him. Smell him. Eat him. Seize his hands and drag him off into the night. Put my head on his shoulder and sleep there until the sun rises and makes the world real again. Does he want to touch me? Is he trying to touch me? If he were trying to touch me he would touch me. If I moved my arm a hair's breadth it would be touching his arm. Should I move my arm? If I moved my arm would he know it was on purpose or would he think it was an accident? *You should definitely, definitely touch me.* I send this message with so much force my eyes cross.

"We could live here," Aurora says sleepily, "and never go home. We could sleep inside a velvet tent and have midnight picnics." Jack strokes the inside of my wrist with his thumb and I nearly startle out of my skin.

"A velvet tent wouldn't be much good against the rain," he says. My fingers rest in his broad palm, and I feel the charge running between us.

"Wherever I go," she says, "it's always summer." After that we are quiet. For the first time in my life I wish Aurora weren't here. I wish I could straddle him, tear off his clothes. Chew away the flesh to the muscle beneath. Rip him open, take him inside. Nothing I have ever felt in my life has readied me for hunger like this. I can smell him: wood, earth, smoke. The stars wheel overhead in their quiet, orderly way. Here they're veiled by the nightglow of the city, but you don't have to go very far out of town before they blaze white and thick across the sky. I want to do everything, everything, everything, but I leave my hand in his and tamp all that desire into a hot coal at the center of my chest. If I never see him again I will definitely go Juliet. Knife to the chest, fade to black. *What is happening to me?* I am not this girl. I am half monster, with spite and bile where normal girls nurture kittens and kind feelings. I do not fall for strangers, do not come unmoored in the dark at a single touch. Already I am cataloguing all the things I would be willing to give up for him if he asked. The night cools and a chill creeps in across the water. It's only when I sit up at last, ready to go back to the car, that I see he's holding Aurora's hand, too.

꧁

When I was smaller, sometimes I wanted my life to be normal. Mom, dad, puppy, two cars. Goldfish in a bowl. Home videos of my first steps. A baby book with my first words written down. School pictures on the fridge, brothers and sisters, curfews. Grandparents. Thanksgiving with a turkey and everyone getting too drunk and fighting, like a family. That's the thing you have to understand: None of this seemed that weird to me, because Cass and Maia had already set the bar high.

After we left Maia's, Cass and I lived a lot of places. I don't remember most of them, or they blur together in my mind, one long series of big kitchens full of people, dirty bathrooms, broken instruments. Wooden floorboards with gaps in between them full of dust, and windows that never kept out the cold. Walls painted haphazardly in weird, clashing colors. The smell of incense. Communal houses, punk houses, hippie houses. Sometimes there were other kids around, but usually I was the only one. We lived in one house for a while with ten other people. A desiccated cat that someone had found in the basement hung on the wall over the fireplace. It used to give me nightmares. Dinner was always a giant pot of Dumpstered vegetables cooked on the stove all day into a tasteless mash. Too many guests. Travelers, punks, maybe sometimes homeless people who'd wandered in off the street. On the weekends, there would be shows in the basement, so loud the house shook. Cass and I had the attic, low-ceilinged but big, and there was a triangle-shaped window at one end that went all the way from the floor to the pitch of the roof. I'd lie next to it for hours, looking out at the street below. Sometimes in the night I'd wake up, shaken out of sleep by the sound of Cass crying in her bed across from mine.

That time didn't last too long. Cass was working two or three jobs at a time, and it was easiest for us to live in a place where other people could take care of me. She'd taught herself to read people's cards and make spells years ago, even before she met Maia. She'd turned out to be good at it, good enough to see other people's lives unwinding in front of them, good enough to untangle the delicate threads of sex and death and money and hope. Our housemates would come to her with their questions, their love problems, their private mysteries and sorrows. I got used to it, dozing late at night in my little bed while Cass held someone's hand, her fingers moving across their palm. Got used to the shirring sound of her tarot cards as she shuffled them, the low raspy murmur of her voice as she spelled out the future. She never asked for money, but people gave it to her, or other gifts if money was something they didn't have. A velvet coat, an antique rosary, muffins, a patchwork bag. Presents for me: colored pencils, drawing paper, my first set of oil paints, the tubes half-spent but still good. I remember squeezing out dabs of color for the first time, the sharp tangy smell that is like no other smell in the world. Touching the vibrant paint and bringing my finger to my mouth for the barest taste.

Cass's name got around and she started reading cards for people with real money, people who lived in new houses all by themselves. Houses with dishwashers and microwaves and carpet. Refrigerators shone white and clean; inside them were cartons of milk and eggs, neatly ordered condiments, the orange juice I wasn't allowed to have because it was too expensive. When Cass took me with her I'd sit and draw quietly in a corner while women with shining hair and perfectly lipsticked mouths asked Cass if their husbands were cheating on them, if their kids would get into good colleges, if they'd find love and, if so, where it would be waiting for them. The most boring questions I could imagine. "So well behaved," they'd say, looking over at me, like I was in a zoo. I didn't understand how people who lived in houses like that could worry about anything at all.

As soon as Cass got enough money together we moved into an apartment of our own, the apartment we live in now. I had my own room, my own window. Our own kitchen—"Dear god," Cass said, when we first moved in, "I thought I'd never see a clean kitchen again"—and our own living room with our own couch. Shabby and small, but it was clean, and it was ours. No guests unless we invited them. No guests really but Aurora, and sometimes men Cass dated for a while, always the same quiet, gentle types who stared moonily at her over the breakfast table and disappeared after a month or two, banished from her orderly macrobiotic world as soon as they got too close. Never, ever Maia. Cass has a guillotine heart, severing ties as neatly as a whistle-sharp blade cutting the head from the body. Like any good revolutionary, she pretends that the casualties mean nothing.

We were still poor. For a while when things were really bad, Cass and I would stand in line at the food bank once a week, where white-haired church ladies handed out yellow bricks of government cheese and big plastic bags of instant oatmeal. There was always a pile of bread, one or two days stale, from a bakery near our apartment, and meat that came in a can with a silhouette of a chicken. I thought they had somehow put a real chicken in there, that you could open the can to find a pet. I cried when Cass said we didn't eat that kind of stuff and handed it back. She'd send me over to Aurora's for dinner, but there was never any food at her house, either. Trips to the grocery store and wholesome meals didn't make it on Maia's to-do list between shooting up and sleeping it off. Half the time, Aurora didn't eat unless she ate with us. All that money might as well have been dust. Sometimes, Maia would get it together enough to hire people to help, but she'd forget to pay them, or they'd end up holing up in her room with her and doing drugs, or one day they'd wander off, and Aurora would be left to run feral again, with only me and Cass to make sure she showed up for school and ate a meal every now and then. When I took Cass's food stamps to the grocery store around the corner, piled up bulk brown rice and oatmeal and sixteen different kinds of vegetables, the lady who always worked the register would sometimes put a bag of Doritos on top of my groceries, hold her finger to her lips, and wink at me.

Aurora and I ran wild young. Cass tried to keep us locked down but gave up quick, settling for exhaustive lectures on the functions and maintenance of the human reproductive system; a crash course in what to do when people got too wasted; and firm exhortations to me to keep myself and Aurora not pregnant, free of disease, and more or less sober. "And *no junk food*," she'd add. Girls at school wanted in on me and Aurora's twinhood, our late nights and freedom, our recklessness and our crazy stories. But those girls didn't understand how good they had it with someone in charge, someone who called the shots, stayed up until they came home, left the porch light on.

I was at a party with Aurora last year. The hosts were friends of friends of people she knew. People who were a lot older than us, and weren't too interested in hiding how much money they had. "Tacky," Aurora hissed, fingering sequin-crusted throw pillows and cashmere blankets tossed over the overstuffed couches. Velvet drapes. Scented candles in gold sconces. Cold cuts on cut-crystal plates. A painting on the wall that turned out, on closer examination, to be a Monet. "Of course, it's one of the lesser-known pieces," said the hostess with false modesty, coming up behind me.

Aurora and I were giggling in a corner when a shrink-wrapped babe stalked over to us. Up close, she was total construct, younger woman stapled on top of old bones. Fake boobs straining her satin dress, chemical-plump mouth. Her eyebrows had that surprised look women get after one too many plastic surgeries. "I know who you are," she said to Aurora, jabbing her with one red-taloned finger. She was very, very drunk. She wobbled there for a moment, glaring at us.

"I don't know you," Aurora said. "Thankfully."

"You know my *husband*," the woman said. Aurora's eyes got big. "You think your pert little ass will get you anything you want. You think you're really something. But you know why men want to fuck little whores like you? Because you're *stupid*." She teetered on her perilous heels and stabbed her finger at us one last time. "Stay away from him," she snarled. She pivoted, nearly overshooting her spin and coming around to face us again, and stalked away.

"Oh my god," Aurora said. We looked at each other and then we both began to laugh. "That was *so weird*," she gasped. "Let's get *out* of here."

I never asked who the husband was. It didn't really matter.

After the night in the park I send out a psychic call. I'm so hooked I hijack a pile of Cass's crystals and leave them under my pillow, willing them to bring him to me, but all they do is give me a stiff neck. Aurora says she has no idea who he is or where he came from. He wouldn't let us give him a ride home from the park, strode off into the darkness before we came to our senses and asked how to find him again. Rockers are a dime a dozen in this town, but he's something else again. I've never heard anyone play music like that.

"You're in love," Aurora says. She thinks it's cute. If she's staking her own claim on him, she's not saying. She's sitting in my kitchen, drinking Dr Pepper that she brought over herself. If Cass is home Aurora puts the soda in a mug. She can't bear, she says, to watch Cass's face when she sees the can. But we're home alone and so an unlit cigarette dangles in her fingers and she runs a thumb around the can's edge between sips.

"I am not in love," I snap. "You can't fall in love with someone you just met."

Aurora rolls her eyes. "Someone's never read a fairy tale."

"We've read all the same fairy tales. This is the real world."

"This is the *real world*. Sure." Her skin glows gold-brown against her white tank top and her clotted tangle of necklaces. She's wearing cutoffs that are barely more than underwear, and under the shirt a tiny crocheted bikini that's so bright I can see it through the fabric like a beacon. "Let's go swimming," she says. "Get your suit."

The beach is crowded with little kids and their parents, basking in the hot afternoon sun, drunk on the glorious summer. We spread our towels, stretch out at the lake's edge. Aurora leaps up, bellowing, runs pell-mell into the water with a crash, and then runs back out again and flings herself on her towel. Dads sit up, shading their eyes with one hand, staring after her long legs and white hair. She rolls around on the towel like a puppy and lies there, panting. "The water's great. We could drive around until we find him."

"I'm sure that would work."

"Probably better than spirit messengers."

"Shut up." I roll over on my stomach, make a show of ignoring her. If you mapped the inside of my brain, it would go like this: his hands, his mouth, his skin, his face, his palm against mine. But I had no idea it was that obvious. Aurora kicks her feet and laughs at her own joke. "Sorry," she says. "I never see you being, like, irresponsible. Less than focused. He's your first boyfriend. It's adorable."

"He's not my fucking boyfriend. I don't even know him."

"You wish he was your boyfriend."

"I don't need a goddamn boyfriend! Jesus. You're such a bitch."

"You love me."

"I do love you."

She stretches her hand across our towels and takes mine, tugs it toward her. I roll over on my side, facing her, and she stares at me with her inscrutable eyes. Like she's going to tell me a secret. Something crucial she found out about love, or sex, or what happens to you when you feel like this and it makes no sense, when someone you've only talked to once takes over your entire brain until you're twitchy with it, until you drop things in the kitchen and turn the stereo up way too loud and think about shaving your head or kicking through a wall or running out into the street and screaming because you can't even stand yourself anymore. She widens her eyes at me and I wait for her to give me the answer.

"I'm starving," she says. "Let's go eat hamburgers."

❧

I work at a fruit stand in the open-air market downtown. It's built on a hill, and underneath the open-air part there are layers of shops clinging to the steep hillside. The street level's made up of long intersecting covered arcades full of stalls: fruit and fish and bread, flowers, ugly tie-dyed hippie clothes. Silver jewelry and amber pendants, bundles of lavender, fuzzy wool pullovers imported from Ecuador next to sandals made out of leather straps and tire rubber.

Crafts for rich people, like handmade wooden children's toys, or flavored jams you buy for relatives you don't know very well that stay unopened in a cupboard for years until someone throws them out. Pierogi and humbow, gyros and hot dogs.

In the winter I love my work. All the out-of-towners flee the eternal damp. We have to wear sweaters and wool hats to keep out the cold, and we drink coffee until we're cracked-out and speedy. The cobblestoned streets are wet and foggy, the low mournful sound of the ferry horn carries across the water, and all the afternoons are dreamy and quiet. I work after school and on weekends, and it's always a relief to come here after the crowded halls and bells marking every hour, pop quizzes on nothing, lunch in the white-tiled cafeteria that reeks of old meatballs. I'd rather be at the market, where the salt smells from the fish stand mingle with the salt smell of the air, and seagulls squawk overhead, and the goth girls at the pierogi stand trade us steaming dumplings for apples and pears.

The lower levels are a maze of high-ceilinged hallways and big windows that look out over the bay. Creaking wooden floorboards, smells of incense and baking and cedar. Tiny shops tucked away around blind corners and in odd nooks. The Egyptian import store, where Aurora and I used to buy silver ankhs and wadjet eyes as Tutankhamun-obsessed girls. The bead store, where we spent hours sifting through wooden trays of colored glass, late-afternoon sun glinting red and blue and green among the beads. And our favorite then, our favorite still: the witch store. Walls of bookshelves to the left of the door, with titles like *Goddess Divination* and *Magickal Herbcraft* and *Following the Moon*.

On the right, shelves and shelves of vitamins and tinctures and incenses and mysterious potions. The light in that shop has a quality to it that is thicker and richer than ordinary light, oozing across the glass bottles and casting shadows among the incense boxes. Cass took me there to buy my first tarot deck, from the long counter with a glass case that runs half the length of the store, full of cards: the Rider Waite and the Crowley Thoth deck, the Osho Zen Tarot, the Russian tarot and the Medieval tarot, goddess tarots, moon tarots, all laid out on swatches of velvet. The counter is cluttered with china bowls filled with beaded bracelets and more incense, pentacle charms, stones with special powers. Jars of rose petals and salts, ceramic Buddhas garlanded with jade, bundles of sage.

I used to be in love with the girl who worked at the witch store when I was a kid. She was elfin but not at all frail, and piled her crow-colored hair on top of her head in complicated knots. Her arms were inky with tattoos, sigils and runes and old woodcut illustrations running from her shoulders to her wrists. She always wore black: black lace dresses cut short and ragged, faded black concert shirts peppered with holes and tight black jeans, black boots or black canvas sneakers. Silver rings on every finger and silver pendants on silver chains.

When Aurora and I were young it was our greatest ambition to someday be the witch-store girl. We spent whole afternoons poking among the boxes of incenses, sneaking glances at her and imagining her life: her apartment filled with altars and candles and tapestries, her bed strewn with crushed-velvet pillows and bits of herbs, her collection of Dead Can Dance and Siouxsie and Clan of Xymox and

This Mortal Coil on vinyl. Probably her boyfriend was one of the other people who worked in the market, one of the fruit-stand boys, equally cool-eyed and mysterious and beautiful. When we bought our vanilla oil and Nag Champa the witch-store girl would ignore us until the last possible minute, ignore even radiant, otherworldly Aurora; she would look out the window with one finger holding her place in her book, which was always a book of spells. I'd stand there twisting one foot behind the other, wanting to ask her if it was possible to move into her life, or even what that life looked like, what she did after work, what she thought about, who she loved, could she tell our fortunes from the pack of tarot cards she kept in her bag with her pot and her clove cigarettes.

These days the witch-store girl is a different girl. I do work in the market, and that life has lost some of its luster now that I'm the one hauling compost after the fruit stand closes, or bantering with the fish-stall boys who love to flirt with everyone, or half freezing to death on the long winter afternoons. Aurora still meets me after work sometimes, though, and we go to the witch store and rummage through books about Wicca and handfasting, or uncap the brown bottles of essential oil and hold them up to each other's noses. The witch-store girl still ignores us.

Summer in the market is hell. Summer is so many tourists you have to kick at them to get anywhere; they gape at everything, take pictures of themselves wearing stupid hats or holding up cups of coffee, like coffee is something they can't get where they are from. They ask you directions to places you've never heard of, or where they should eat dinner, or where they should stay, or if their car will be okay where they left it, while their sticky-faced children knock apples off the displays and wail in hellish chorus. In the summers I work full-time, and sometimes by the end of the day I never want to see another human being again.

Today has been a long day full of tourists palming peaches in their meaty hands, and I'm tired. I'm working with Raoul, who is my favorite. He's a poet and he's even meaner than me. He makes fun of the tourists to their faces and they love it, not realizing he's serious. He lives in a studio apartment down the street from the market, and after work he lets me come over and smoke pot out of his hookah and fall asleep on his couch with his cat. His cat is named Oscar Wilde and its fur is the color and softness of dandelions gone to seed. Behind me I can hear the fish-stall boys yelling and chanting. The tourists cheer as they hurl fish back and forth.

"The peaches here come highly recommended," someone says. I look up, ready to make a smart-aleck remark, and it's Jack. I want to reach across the fruit and touch him, see if he's real.

"You," I say, and he smiles.

"I've been looking for you."

I open my mouth. Nothing comes out. I close it again.

"Are you doing anything after work?"

"I get off in half an hour."

"Can I come and get you?"

"Yeah," I say. Trying not to squeak. He grins at me, tips an imaginary cap. Vanishes back into the crowd.

"Who was *that*," Raoul says.

"Some boy I met at one of Aurora's parties."

"My goodness," Raoul says. "Next time, invite me."

I drop an entire flat of plums before I leave, and Raoul laughs at me. When I pick up my backpack at the end of my shift my hands are shaking. Jack's waiting for me down the street, leaning against a wall, one booted foot tucked behind the other. I hold up a bag of peaches and he smiles. People turn their heads to look at him as they walk past. He leads me to a motorcycle parked down the block and hands me a helmet. "Do you have to be anywhere?" he says.

"No."

"Good. Have you ever ridden on one of these?" I shake my head. "Just hold on." He throws one long leg over the back of the bike. I put the helmet on. My body fits neatly behind his. He takes both my wrists and pulls my arms tight around his waist. I can feel the muscles of his back moving against my chest. The bike roars to life, and for a moment I can see the possibility of my entire life, the story waiting to be written.

We drive for a long time, through the city and through miles of suburbs with their identical streets cluttered with identical houses and identical stores selling identical objects, out onto the long country roads that wind through farmland and sun-dappled woods. Overhead the green-leaved branches meet to make a latticework ceiling as we hurtle westward. I can feel every movement of his body. The wind tears merrily at my clothes, fluttering my shirt against my ribcage. At last the trees thin and ahead I can see a line of blue-grey. He's taken us all the way to the Pacific.

He parks the bike and we walk through the trees to a stony beach littered with driftwood. It's late in the day, but the sun-bleached trunks hold the sun's heat. I sit next to him, our backs against a log, our legs stretching out toward the water. Great green waves crash against the tideline and I can hear pebbles clattering as the water sucks back out to sea. Underneath the pebbles is another, different sound, like music, but nothing I could recognize or name.

I know how to draw, and I know how to kiss, and I know how to put fabrics next to each other in a way that makes their richness clearer, or arrange a line of glass jars on a windowsill so that they catch the light in a way you would not expect. I know how to run for a long time, head down, knees pumping. I know how to see beauty in other things, but I have never taken much time to see any beauty in myself. I am to Aurora what a gift-store postcard print is to a Klimt hanging on the museum wall. I do not love her any less for it; I think it is best to know what you are and make peace with it. I like myself, but I do not have any illusions about what I am. *Why me?* I want to say to him, but if I ask he might start to wonder himself, and out of all the beautiful things in my life he is already the most extraordinary. He takes a knife out of his pocket and cuts a piece of peach and puts it in my mouth, licks the rivulets of juice from his wrist cat-quick, cuts me another piece. The soft felt of the peach skin is hot, the flesh cool and sweet beneath. I bite his thumb and hold it there in my mouth and he sets aside the peach and the knife and puts his other hand in my hair and kisses me.

Kissing him is like falling into a river, some great fierce current carrying me outside of my body, and all around us the music of the water rises and rises, and I can hear the wind moving over the sand, the distant singing of the stars veiled behind their curtain of blue sky, the slow, resonant chords of the earth turning on its axis. And then the music is gone again and he is only another human, kissing me on a warm beach. His mouth tastes of peaches and his skin smells like the sea. Everything feels real and more than real: the softness of his mouth, the hard pebbles beneath me, the warm wood against my back, the heat of his skin. The sand-papery stubble on his cheeks rubs my chin pink. We kiss until my mouth feels bee-stung and full and all the muscles in my body go liquid, until my knees shake and I know I won't be able to stand up again without help. He kisses my cheeks, my eyelids, my earlobe, the place where my neck curves into my shoulder. I touch the hollow of his throat and he takes my hand in his, moves his mouth away from mine, kisses my knuckles, opens my fingers and presses his mouth into my palm. The wind coming off the water is colder now. I put my head on his chest and close my eyes and let the thunder of his heartbeat echo through me until it erases my thoughts one by one and there is nothing left but the sound of him.

It wasn't like we didn't know there were rules. Or, I mean, I knew that, at least. Maybe Aurora didn't. It was more like rules were a thing for other people. Like you could be a girl, and it meant dressing in a way that made you pretty and soft. It meant not saying things you weren't supposed to say, and knowing what those things were. It meant being quiet if you were smart, humble if you were pretty. It meant when boys asked you to touch your elbows behind your back you'd giggle and do it as if you didn't know what they were trying to see.

Aurora always said everything, anything, from the very beginning. Aurora knew she was beautiful, knew she was smarter than everyone around her except me. Knew she was rich, knew she could do whatever the fuck she wanted and no one, nothing, would ever be able to stop her. Aurora was fierce, funny, mean. Aurora and I learned to smoke together, stole our first sips of whisky out of Maia's prodigious stash, cussed in class, sealed ourselves in. Aurora and I made a world for two, a secret club that wasn't a secret because everyone outside us saw the two of us together and knew we lived in a country whose borders they couldn't cross. We didn't care that people hated us, didn't care that no one ever called us after school or invited us to slumber parties. We had no interest in dipping our classmates' hands into bowls of water while they slept to see if we could make them pee, or playing Light as a Feather, Stiff as a Board with girls whose faces closed up tight when they looked at us. We partied with adults, not little girls.

I had friends who weren't Aurora, early on. I remember this girl I knew in grade school, this girl Tracy, the most normal name and the most normal girl. Her house had a room we weren't allowed to go in and all the furniture was covered in plastic sheeting. Her mom made us snacks and we played games in her front yard. Hopscotch and running through a sprinkler in the afternoons when it was warm enough. She had a shelf of dolls in her pink room and all the dolls had dresses. She had a child-sized wooden kitchen, a fake wood stove with burners painted on, an oven with a door that opened. We would make cookies you couldn't see in a metal bowl that used to be in her real kitchen. It took me a while to catch on. The cookies were pretend. The whole thing was a game. Tracy's house had cabinets filled with real cookies in packages. Tracy's house had white walls and clean blue carpet and a walkway to the front door made out of round pebbles set in cement. Brown beds on either side were planted with petunias at precisely measured one-foot intervals.

My house never smelled like Tracy's house. My house smelled like incense and patchouli and sage and candles burning and soup on the stove in a big pot, and sometimes like weed when Cass had a boyfriend. My house had crooked windows and mismatched curtains Cass pieced together out of scraps. Creaky wooden floors, a bathroom full of chipped tiles, baseboards Cass had to continually tack back to the walls. My house had crumbling terracotta pots bursting over with herbs and tendrilly, disordered houseplants. Piles of records in the corners and books spilling from their shelves onto the floor, the couch, the kitchen table. Set lists and fliers from old punk and hardcore shows that Cass and Maia used to steal every time they went out to a club. Old medical posters and anatomy books, a plastic model of a human torso with transparent skin and multicolored organs. Tracy wasn't allowed to come over to my house.

Tracy's house. I liked it, but I didn't like it. Tracy's house was a different planet, a planet with order and strict scheduling. Tracy always had the newest Barbies, which she handed down to her younger sister as more current models were released. We ate dinner at the same time every night there, and we had cereal from a box in the mornings unless

I slept over on the weekend, and then her mom would make us toast with holes cut out of the center and an egg where the bread had been. Once her mom asked if I wanted to go to church with them and I said okay, and so they took me in their van that smelled like old fast food with her brothers and her sister strapped in the back. Tracy gave me one of her dresses to wear, and I remember it had ruffles and the collar left a red mark on my neck. At church her family sang a lot of different songs they already knew the words to. Tracy liked a boy a grade ahead of us who left her a chocolate bar in her desk. They were going out. "Where do you go?" I asked, and she looked at me funny. Right away I knew that was the wrong question, but I didn't know why. Cass let me go anywhere I wanted. I kissed Tracy's boyfriend inside a tractor tire on the elementary-school playground. Three times. On the third time, I let him put his hand up my shirt. I never told Tracy. Afterward when he passed me in the hall he would look at his friends on either side and they would cover their mouths with their hands and laugh.

Cass never cut my hair and it grew in brown tangles down my back until the year I started seventh grade, when I cut it myself with Cass's sewing scissors in our kitchen. That was the year Tracy and I decided not to be friends anymore. We never talked about it; it just happened. We had only been friends in the first place because Cass needed somewhere for me to go after school. That was when she was still washing dishes in a restaurant. She'd come home late, smelling like fryer grease and cigarette smoke, and I'd rub her back and tell her about Tracy's cookies that weren't real, and she'd laugh. I didn't know why it was funny, but I always laughed, too.

I knew we were poor, but it wasn't a thing I could explain. Other people explained it for me. They'd pull my hair and tell me it was dirty, or they'd tell me my clothes were wrong. Tracy's mom gave me a bag of Tracy's old clothes with a sanctimonious smile, but everything Tracy wore was ugly and didn't fit. Looking at that sad pile of pink frillery filled me with a sick, unnameable shame. I took the bag home and stuffed it in the back of my closet. Cass found it months later and asked me what it was, and when I told her, she cried, and I didn't have to go over to Tracy's anymore. After that, it was me and Aurora, sisters and twins, the way it always should have been. After Tracy, Cass didn't try to stop me from spending all my time at Maia's, running around past bedtime with Aurora, who'd figured out a million ways to get into trouble before she figured out anything else.

I know the first time I see him that Jack isn't who I'm supposed to love. Too old, trouble. Musician. We're wary of musicians, in my family. My family being Cass and Aurora and me. Musicians get famous and cry about it. They knock you up and bail. Musicians are on heroin. They mope around. Musicians: seriously not worth the investment of your time and energy. You always have to pay their rent— this is what Cass has told me—until they make it, and then they leave you for a swimsuit model. Or else they die. "What about girl musicians?" Aurora asked once.

"Girl musicians, too," Cass said, and got that face she gets when she is done talking. "You want to date, baby girls, go for accountants."

But that's not how it happens when your heart gets in the middle. Jack is like a light turned on in a room I didn't even know was dark. It's always been Aurora who's loved boys with danger written under their skin. Until now, I've never loved anyone except Aurora. It's more than his music, more even than the smell of his skin. More than the way his body is like a magnet calling all the iron in my blood. He's a drug that's hooked me on the very first trip. I knew it, the first time he kissed me, knew I was caught. Who am I, to fight the hand of fate? I already know what happens to people who tell the gods how to do their job.

⁓

When I get home from the ocean Aurora is asleep in my bed and Cass is gone. The apartment is quiet and cool. Aurora is curled tightly in on herself, her arms crossed on her chest. I tuck the blanket around her shoulders. She makes a soft anguished noise in her sleep and then opens her eyes, staring at me without seeing. "He's here," she says. I walk to the window and look out. The street is empty.

"There's no one," I say, but then I see a shadow that is darker than all the other shadows and at its center a spark of red. Like the skeleton man's eyes, the man from Aurora's party. I close the curtains. "He can't get in."

"Who can't get in?" Aurora asks behind me. She sits up, blinking. "Who are you talking to?"

"No one. Never mind." I climb into the bed and put my head in her lap and she tangles her fingers in my hair, smoothing it away from my face.

"You smell like boy." She squirrels down next to me and I tuck my chin against her shoulder. "Tell me everything," she says, and I tell her.

"You like him."

"I like him."

"Don't go away from me," she whispers. "Everybody goes away from me."

"I'm not going anywhere." The curtains move although there is no wind. Everything else has gone still. I close my eyes and all I can see is him: his face, his eyes, his hands with the knife, cutting into the peach. His hands on my skin. "I'm not going anywhere," I say again, this time less certain. I put my arm around Aurora, curl up against the curve of her back, and wait for dawn.

In the morning the world seems ordinary again. I leave Aurora asleep and pad into the kitchen, where Cass is at our scarred wooden table with a tarot spread in front of her and her hands around her favorite chipped blue mug. The kitchen is so familiar, so shabby and un-mysterious. This is our apartment, the ancient green stove whose left burners only work when they have a mind to, the tangle of houseplants in their net hammocks dangling from the ceiling, trailing leafy streamers down the cheery yellow walls. There are the wooden shelves lined with mason jars full of Cass's herbs and roots and flowers. If I opened the cupboards I would find plates that don't match, jam jars doing double duty as water glasses, mugs from the Salvation Army that say things like WORLD'S #1 TEACHER and FORTY AND LOVING IT! I can smell bread baking. Nothing sinister could possibly happen in this kitchen. I pour myself a cup of coffee, the one vice Cass allows, and sit at the table, tucking my feet up underneath me. Cass looks tired, the lines around her grey eyes more pronounced. She stares at the cards, chewing on her lip.

"You look like Fate is not on your side this morning," I say.

"I was asking about Maia. It never changes much." She sweeps the cards into a pile, shuffles them, puts them away in their carved wooden box, and shakes herself. "Let's talk about happier things." I can't stop the smile that spreads across my face.

"I met a boy." Boy is the wrong word. She laces her long fingers together.

"A *boy*," she echoes.

"At Aurora's party. He was playing music in the garden. It was—I'd never—" I falter. I can't describe what happened that night when Jack played. "It was better than anything I have ever heard. And then he talked to me, and yesterday we went to the ocean after I got off work, and we had a picnic." Describing it in our homely kitchen makes it seem as though what's happening to me is ordinary, too. I am a girl, it is summer. I like a boy. In the fall I will start school again. There is no room for skeleton men in this kitchen, no place for songs that are like spells. For a moment I can stop thinking about Jack's mouth. But Cass's eyes are serious now.

"Be careful," she says.

"I will."

"You don't know him."

"It feels like I do." Is that true? I don't know. Something in me recognizes something in him. His body brings my body home. If that's not a kind of knowing, I don't need to know what knowing is.

She sighs and runs her hands through her hair. There is grey in it now, which still surprises me. Cass has always seemed barely older than I am. She refuses to dye her hair dark again, which I think is funny, considering how many unnatural colors it was when she was younger. "That's a different kind of vanity," she'd said when I pointed that out. "I'm not afraid of growing up."

Now she scowls at me. "That's always how it feels."

"This is different."

"You're seventeen. You think everything is different when you're seventeen. How old is he? What does he do?"

"He's a musician." I ignore the first question.

"Stay away from musicians."

"Don't worry."

"Of course I worry. I let you do whatever you want, I let you grow up without—" She stops. She had been about to say *without a father.* "I let you run around with Aurora," she says instead. "Be careful." Her face is impossible to read.

"I promise."

"Is someone baking bread?" Aurora asks from the doorway. She's sleepy-eyed and tousled, her shirt slipping off one shoulder, her white hair disordered.

"It should be about done," Cass says, and gets up to check the oven. Aurora takes a mug out of a cabinet, pours the last of the coffee. She has never commented on the fact that my house has four rooms and hers has forty, or that you can see the floorboards through our fraying rugs, or that nearly all the beautiful things we own are things Aurora bought for us. She gave me a Kiki Smith print for my birthday last year that's worth more than everything else in our house put together.

"God, I had the weirdest dream," she says, sitting down.

"What did you dream?" Cass asks.

"I was being chased by this man, and his eyes were made out of fire, and he wanted something from me but I didn't know what it was. I was running through this weird apartment with all these windows and on the walls were these terrible paintings of people being tortured, and everywhere there was this music and it was getting louder and louder. And all I wanted was to stop and go to sleep there and forget everything, but I knew if I stopped the man would never let me leave again." As she talks a cloud moves across the sun and the light in the kitchen dulls. Cass closes her eyes, reaches forward, touches Aurora's forehead with two fingers. She whispers something, opens her eyes, takes her hand away.

"I'll make you some tea." She takes away Aurora's coffee mug. Aurora makes a noise of protest as Cass pours the coffee down the drain and sets the kettle on the stove.

"Humor her," I say.

Cass takes jars down from her shelves, measures out herbs. "Will you tell me if you have that dream again?" Like me, she's trying to keep her words light, but I know she is as unnerved as I am.

"Sure," Aurora says, yawning. "Can I have a little coffee?"

"Later," Cass says.

"It was like I wanted the man to catch me, though," Aurora says. "In the dream. Like I knew he could give me something in return, for whatever it was he was going to take, and I wanted to know what it was. There was something beautiful about him, too. The whole thing felt so real."

"It's a mask," Cass says quietly with her back to us. "Beauty like that is always a mask."

"It was a dream," Aurora says. "Can I have some bread, at least?"

Later, after Aurora goes home, and Cass takes her cards and her crystals and her charts and goes to meet a client, I try to draw Jack. I rifle through my records and put on the Gits, smooth the blank sheet of paper with my palms, get out my pencils, arrange and rearrange them, pick them up and put them down again. Whenever I close my eyes all I see is him. I draw a line and it's wrong, another line and it's worse, turn the paper over, try again. I can see him in my mind but not with my hands. Everyone at the party had moved toward him when he played, unseeing, their mouths open, their eyes blank. My work does not have that kind of power, or anything close. There is no magic in anything I ever draw; only labor, and love, and sometimes a grace that becomes larger than the paper or the canvas, so that you can see for a moment the person inside as though they are about to speak to you or come alive. But that does not happen very often, and most of the time my pictures are only pictures, and a lot of the time they are not very good at all. I put the pencil down. I don't want to draw him. I want him here, in my room, his hands across my skin again, his mouth. I want him to play me songs. I want to tangle my fingers in his hair. I want things that make me blush. It is unseemly, I think, to want someone this much. I can't draw what I'm seeing. I would have an easier time trying to draw the shape of a cloud moving across the sky.

I draw a line instead, a line of trees that becomes a dark wood with eyes peering out of it, shadows moving through the trees, dark shapes flitting from one branch to another. The afternoon shades into evening, and my room dims. The figures in the trees seem to move without my drawing them, as though they have taken on a life of their own, reaching out to me, whispering my name. I can see into a world without sunlight, a darkness so dense I can shape it with my hands. My bare feet are on a rough dirt path through the trees and the air has gone cold. Thick vines bristling with thorns wrap around the trunks, a viscous sap dark as blood running down the bark where the thorns have pierced it. The darkness around me is alive, creaking and rustling. The branches of the trees are bare and dry as bones. I hug myself, shivering. I am at the river again, the river in my dream. It gleams with a dull sheen as though it were made out of oil. I am looking for someone. Someone I must find, before it is too late. I can hear the dogs howling. A figure steps onto the path between me and the river, a darkness blacker even than the darkness around it, and it speaks my name aloud in the dark and reaches its arms toward me. I scream and jerk backward, and my room floods with light from the hallway, and I hear my name again, over and over, Cass running through the open door. The darkness is an ordinary darkness again, my own small room with the lights off, my unmade bed, my stereo, my windowsill lined with candles and dried flowers, the disintegrating rag rug underneath my feet. "I didn't hear you come home."

"I thought you were asleep, and then I heard you scream."

"I was drawing." I turn to my desk to show her the forest but the paper is blank.

She lets go of me and walks into the kitchen. I wonder

how long I was in that forest. Where that forest was. Cass brings me a steaming mug of something bitter and sharp-smelling. I climb into my bed without taking off my clothes and she sits with me while I drink the tea, stroking my fore-head, and when I fall asleep at last I do not dream again.

～

"You have got it bad," Raoul says. I'm so dopey with lust I've been tripping over fruit crates all day. We're sitting in the street behind the stand now, on a smoke break, watch-ing the fish-stall boys chuck salmon. They look good and they know it. They're like a tribe of Norsemen, all bulging muscles and piercing blue eyes. Tourist ladies are always trying to get their pictures taken with the handsomest ones. Not so much my speed, but I like to watch Raoul flirt with them. Across the street, the pierogi girls are reading each other's palms. Occasionally the summer breeze brings me a whiff of their patchouli.

Raoul is wearing tight black leather pants, despite the summer sun, and a black tank top that hangs soft and loose and shows off his tattoos and the wooden rosary I've never seen him without. Me, threadbare black T-shirt, black jeans, black boots. The fish-stall boys call us the vampire twins. "Vampires be happy!" the one with the green hat likes to shout at us. "Cheer up, vampires!"

"You don't even know," I say now. I want to fling myself across something but I settle for flailing my arms. "He's, like, I don't even know. Oh my god."

"Like so good he takes away your capacity for intelligent speech," Raoul suggests.

"Shut up." I pretend to chuck a peach at him.

"He's pretty hot."

"Right? But it's more than that. He has this, like, power. Like a magnet. I wish you could have seen him play."

"A magnet. Wow. That must be so compelling."

"You're impossible."

"What do you talk about?"

I blush. "Um. Not a whole lot, so far."

"Ah, yes. The magnet."

"You are such a dick."

"I would never malign the power of the magnet." He stubs out his cigarette on the bottom of his boot and tucks the butt in the compost pile.

"Raoul."

"What?" he says, a portrait of innocence. "Just doing my part for the earth."

After work I follow Raoul home like a puppy. He heats up tamales, and I eat mine with my fingers. Raoul eats his tamales with a pair of chopsticks and turns on MTV.

"When I was little I thought everyone's best friend's aunts and uncles were in music videos," I tell him.

"Yeah? That's kind of weird."

"You want weird, try being Aurora."

Raoul's apartment is much smaller than mine, one room with a tiny bathroom and a tinier kitchen. He's covered the walls with velvet and dried roses and white Christmas lights, crucifixes and paintings of saints. On a table sits a big wooden Virgen de Guadalupe surrounded by candles and flowers and ceramic skulls and rosaries, crystals and cones of incense and miniature bottles of liquor. He has a Pendleton blanket folded on his bed, triangles of color that repeat themselves mosaiclike, and an old acoustic guitar his father gave him. I am not allowed to touch the blanket. When Raoul looks at it his face glows.

I often wonder what it is like for Raoul here, in this city where white people spring everywhere from the damp earth like fungi, but I never ask. I love Raoul because he does not treat me like a teenager, and because he is funny and kind and wise, and because he makes me weird techno mixtapes, stuff like Autechre and Orbital and Plaid, the Chemical Brothers, Carl Craig. I know his family lives in Arizona, and he grew up in the desert, and he spoke Spanish before he spoke English, and he is teaching himself Navajo, which his dad never spoke at home because he got beaten at the boarding school for using it when he was a kid. But that's about all Raoul's told me about his life before he came here. I know he misses living somewhere the sky is so big it makes you feel like a speck of dust, and I know his mom sends him mole sometimes, because when she does he makes chicken in mole and it is so good it almost makes me cry. Oscar Wilde jumps in my lap, angling for tamale. "Uh-uh," I say, pushing him away, and he flicks his tail at me in disdain. Raoul smiles.

MTV is playing hair metal, and we laugh at the outfits. "I need me some of that," Raoul says, when the singer prances across the screen in a leopard vest. I imagine Raoul shirtless in a fur vest, deliberately overcharging tourists for their plums. It's a glorious picture. When I get up to go home Raoul stops me. "You be careful with those older boys," he says. His voice is teasing but his eyes are serious. I think of Cass in our kitchen with those same eyes. When all the adults in your life are telling you the same thing, I know you're supposed to pay attention. But you know what Aurora says? *The hard way is my favorite way to learn.*

Ꮬ

When Aurora and I were little girls we slit open our palms in the room where her father died, pressed our hands together. *Palm to palm is holy palmer's kiss.* We were clumsy with the knife and cut too deep, and the blood ran down our arms and fell in fat red droplets to the floor. We both still have the scars, matching white slashes, and if you push aside the rug in that room you can see where the blood left a stain.

When we were fourteen, Aurora almost died, too. We were drinking Maia's bourbon and watching a movie. I fell asleep, woke with a start when the credits began. Aurora wasn't there. I wandered the whole house looking for her before I thought to go outside. She was lying facedown in the grass, her skin cold, her face in a puddle of her own vomit. When the paramedics came, they said if I had found her any later there would have been nothing they could have done. "What were you *thinking*?" I asked her, when she woke up in the hospital with tubes coming out of her nose. Even like that she was beautiful.

"I thought I could see him if I got far enough toward the other side," she said. I didn't have to ask who she meant.

"Aurora," I said, and then I didn't know what to say after that. She looked at me and her eyes were very old.

"I guess it runs in the family," she said. Only much later did it occur to me I hadn't even thought to call either of our mothers. It was the hospital that called Maia. She'd shown up disheveled and confused, and she held my hand in the hospital room while Aurora slept. "I'm so sorry, baby," she'd whispered, over and over again, until finally I asked her to stop. I'd told the paramedics I was Aurora's sister. I never told Cass about it at all.

After that I tried not to get drunk around Aurora. One of us would always have to know when to stop, and I understood after that night that it was never going to be her. One of us had to learn how to say no, figure a way out, count the exits. It was up to me to keep her safe. There was no one else who could.

❧

"Come over," Aurora says. "Jack's here." I'm trying to draw him again and it's not working. When the phone rang I thought I would jump straight out of my skin.

"Jack's at your house?"

"Uh-huh. Want me to pick you up?"

"Why is Jack at your house?"

"You're right. We should go somewhere. You want pho?"

I give up. "Yeah, sure."

I could change my clothes but that would be weird, because he has only ever seen me in the same clothes. So if I changed them it would be obvious I changed them for him. But maybe he wouldn't know, since he's only seen me twice. But even if he doesn't know, Aurora will, and if she knows I changed my clothes she will know it is more than liking him. She'll know how much I like him, that I really, really like him, and if he is already hers and not mine I don't want her to know. I take off my shirt and stare at myself in the mirror over the dresser. I look like myself with no shirt. Pale soft belly, pale soft breasts in the worn-thin sports bra I wear to hide them, broad shoulders heavy with muscle. I put the shirt back on. Maybe I need a different shirt. But all my shirts look the same. From the back I look like a boy. From the front, too, if I am being honest with myself. *Oh my god*, I think, stricken. *What if my entire life I have looked like a hideously ugly boy and everyone loves me too much to tell me.* My face in the mirror is filled with panic. Maybe Jack prefers girls who look like girls. Maybe Jack was confused when he came and got me at the market, was hoping I would lead him to Aurora, with her sylph's body and veil of white hair. Maybe kissing me was a pit stop on the way to the finish line. Maybe they are having sex, like, right now. Maybe even if they are he will still have sex with me. But what if I need a different shirt. If there were something in my room I could hit myself over the head with, I would do that. Before this week I had only two worries: Don't let Aurora kill herself, and don't let Cass find out how messed up Aurora is. Now the spectrum of things to be anxious about has exploded into a full-scale rainbow.

I hear Aurora's honk in the street below my window and I grab my bag and run downstairs. I forgot to leave a note for Cass, but I can call her if we're out late. Jack turns around in the passenger seat of the car as I climb into the backseat and gives me a long, greedy kiss. "Gross," Aurora says peaceably as she drives. When Jack lets me go I'm breathless and flustered.

"Hi," I say, running my hands down my jeans. "What were you guys up to?" Aurora meets my eyes in the rear-view mirror and winks. Jack winds one long arm behind his seat, brushes his fingers against my knee. I am mortified by the effect this gesture has on me, stare resolutely out the window, try to gather some semblance of dignity as a rich glow spreads between my legs. Maybe Aurora will pull the car over right now and go for a walk. A really long walk. Maybe Jack will take off all his clothes.

"I want pho," Aurora says, her raspy voice reeling me back to a world where everyone is wearing clothes and having an ordinary conversation about dinner. If Raoul could see inside my head right now he would die laughing. I send him a psychic message. *Raoul. Help. Is. This. Normal.*

"What's pho?" Jack asks.

"Oh my *god*," Aurora says. "How do you not know this glory? Noodles in broth with cow parts. And they bring you a cream puff with your order."

"What kind of cow parts," Jack says.

"Like all the parts. You can get tofu and vegetable if you're going to be a baby."

"I just like to know what parts, before I make a commitment."

I'm quiet as they banter. Aurora's playing Aphex Twin, the ambient stuff, pulsing and spooky. The streetlights flash by. There is this sense of expectation that fills the car, like before everything was one way, and now everything is going to be another. We're driving into the night where everything begins. Jack touches my knee again and I take his hand. He rubs one thumb across my knuckles, and if I weren't sitting down already I'd fall over. "Let's go to California," I say.

"Now?" Aurora's excited. I can see her perk up. "We should get coffee first."

"I'm supposed to work tomorrow night," Jack says.

"Quit." Aurora bounces in her seat. "I'll drive. It's only eight hours to the border. We can wake up on the beach."

"They have a beach in this state, too," Jack points out.

"It's not the same beach."

"It's the same ocean."

"Only technically."

"In California you can sleep on the beach without freezing to death," I say.

"Even in the winter," Aurora adds. "In Southern California."

"We could call your work and say we kidnapped you," I offer. "We're holding you for ransom."

"I think they might just fire me."

"That works fine," Aurora says. "Because then you wouldn't have to worry about your job." We're at the pho place now. She circles the block a few times, finds a parking spot down the street. Jack unfolds himself from the car. I get out, and he pulls me to him again. "Hey, you," he says into my ear.

"Get a room!" Aurora yells. "Or I'll eat your fucking noodles!"

Inside, we order soup. The waiter is even younger than we are. He brings us cream puffs in paper wrappers. Aurora tears hers in half, licks out the cream at the center. "You got some on your nose," Jack says, and leans forward to wipe it away with his thumb. Aurora beams at him. I tear apart basil and cilantro and heap them on my noodles, stir in plum sauce, don't look up until he leans back in his seat again. Aurora dumps in half the bottle of chili sauce, gets to work with her chopsticks. She always eats like it's her last meal. I try to be dainty for Jack's benefit, but I am not graceful under the best of circumstances, and I give up quickly. Aurora sings under her breath, a line about driving down the coast at night. It's from one of her dad's songs.

Without warning I'm seized by happiness so huge I want to jump up and hug them both. *This is my life*, I think, *these are my friends.* Jack is a mystery, but he's my mystery, smiling at me now like we both know a secret that's too good to keep to ourselves. There's Aurora, shoveling noodles into her mouth, licking chili sauce off her fingers: the most beautiful girl in the world, but also the funniest and the most generous and the easiest to love. The air is that kind of warm where you feel like you're floating, and I'm full and my Vietnamese iced coffee is thick and sweet but not too sweet, and Jack is holding my hand under the table. Everyone in the restaurant keeps turning to look at us. Summer is happening, and our whole lives are in front of us, and here we are, making a circle out of love.

Later, Aurora drives us back to her house. I call Cass and tell her I'm sleeping over. "Okay," she says, yawning into the phone. "See you in the morning. Tell Aurora I'll do her chart this week if she wants." Aurora is privately dubious when it comes to Cass's magical powers, but she takes Cass's astrological advice like it's straight gospel. I'm more skeptical. Getting life advice from your mom is always a bad call anyway, even if technically it's coming from space rocks.

Aurora wants to watch *The Abyss*. We pile into her bed like puppies. I stretch out between the two of them and they curl into me, Jack's arm around my shoulders, Aurora's head on my chest. I run my fingers through her hair and she dozes until the alien tongue of water makes its way through the cabin to say hello. That's her favorite part. When Coffey shuts the hatch on it and it collapses in a giant wave, she turns her face up to Jack. "I like you," she says sleepily. "You can stay. But if you fuck with my sister, I'll slit your throat in your sleep."

"Stay frosty," he says, and she opens her eyes wide.

"Wow," she says to me. "This one, you must keep." I hug them closer. We fall asleep like that in her big soft bed, tangled up in one another, and when the white light of morning wakes me I can't tell where my body ends and their bodies begin.

When Jack leaves in the afternoon Aurora makes us Cup O' Noodles and milkshakes—about all she can manage in the kitchen—and we go back to bed. She flips through channels until she finds an *X-Files* marathon. "*Wicked,*" she says.

"Oh my god," I say, "this one is so scary." It's the episode where Mulder and Scully are in the woods. They hike in to investigate the mysterious disappearance of a timber crew and end up trapped in a cabin with a dying generator and an ecoterrorist. At night, clouds of minuscule bugs come down out of the sky and mummify anyone who strays outside the circle of the cabin's light. I've never seen alien bugs when I'm hiking, but it's not an entirely inaccurate portrayal of the peninsula. I love it out there, but those woods aren't what I would call friendly.

"This one rules so hard," Aurora says, slurping noodles.

"My baby girls." Maia's standing in the doorway, leaning against the frame.

"Hi, Maia," Aurora says, without looking away from the TV.

"Who spent the night?"

"Oh," I say, "sorry, we should have asked." It makes me feel better to pretend sometimes that Maia is a normal parent, a functional human with concerns like those of other humans with offspring. Is my daughter home safe, is my daughter fed, is my daughter opening the door of our house to strange men. Et cetera.

"You know I don't care," Maia says, coming over to sit on the edge of Aurora's bed. "I like to meet your friends."

"Ssssssh," Aurora says. It's a tense scene. Mulder and Scully and the ecoterrorist stare at the sole remaining light bulb flickering dimly in the cabin. The edges of the dark teem with bugs. The generator coughs.

"When was the last time you ate real food?" Maia asks.

"The last time you bought some," Aurora snaps.

Maia presses a hand to her chest, pretending to have been shot, and rolls her eyes. She's looking pretty good today. Black hair washed and glossy, eyes bright. More or less dressed: ragged flannel shirt that's way too big for her and must have been Aurora's dad's, leggings, Converse. You can mistake her for a teenager until you look in her eyes.

The episode cuts to a commercial. Aurora sucks noodles into her mouth, chugs the last of the salty broth. Cass once made me read the list of ingredients on a Cup O' Noodles aloud. "I want you to picture that *inside your body*," she'd said. I chew contentedly on a salty cube of rehydrated carrot. Mmmmmm.

"So who was that?"

"This boy I'm kind of seeing," I say. "I think." Blushing. Like a teenager. Which I am. But still.

"Her boyfriend," Aurora amends.

"He is not my boyfriend."

"He is definitely your boyfriend."

"I don't have a goddamn boyfriend!"

"Is he dreamy?" Maia asks.

"He's a musician."

Maia laughs. "Does Cass know?"

"Yeah. She's kind of not stoked."

"I'm sure. Where'd you meet him? A show?"

"Here, actually. At Aurora's party. He played in the yard."

"You had a party?" Aurora's watching a commercial for tampons as if it's the most fascinating thing she's ever seen. "Why didn't you tell me you had a party?"

"You were at the party, Maia," I say cautiously. "We talked. Remember?"

"Was I?" She doesn't seem surprised. "Aurora, which party was it?"

Aurora doesn't answer. She chews on the edge of her Styrofoam cup, pats around next to her for her cigarettes without moving her eyes from the screen. "You know you're not supposed to smoke in here," Maia adds. Aurora rolls her eyes, an unconscious echo of Maia, but doesn't answer. I never tell Aurora, because she goes from placid to enraged in the space of a single sentence, but they're so alike it's comical sometimes.

"It was just a few people," I say, although this isn't at all true. "You probably weren't downstairs for very long." I fight the urge to reach over and push up one sleeve of Maia's flannel shirt, check for red lines tracking down her brown skin. It's not like there's anything I can do. Aurora finds her cigarettes, sticks one in her mouth, lights it without looking away from the television.

"Baby," Maia says, and takes it out of her mouth. "Come on."

"Jesus," Aurora mutters, throwing herself back into the pillows with an exaggerated sigh. Maia stretches like a cat. You can still see it in her, the magic Aurora's inherited, that tangible haze of sex and glamour. Even the drugs and sadness haven't ravaged it out of her. She clambers over me and burrows between us. Aurora makes an annoyed noise but relents, puts an arm around Maia's shoulders. The commercials end and we're back to the forest. Mulder and Scully are going to make a run for it. Rain pours down. The road out of the woods is a mess of mud and water. The bugs gather. I know how it ends, but I still hold my breath.

"Do they make it?" Maia asks.

"Oh my god," Aurora says. "Seriously. Shut *up*."

Jack invites us to come see him play at the OK Hotel. The club is already packed when we get there. Crow-haired goth girls in rosaries and lace dresses lean against the bar, surrounded by boys in leather and spikes and big boots, tattoos snaking up their arms. Aurora is wearing white, as always, a silk slip from the forties edged in fraying lace, rhinestone clips holding her hair away from her face, dusty old brown cowboy boots. In the gloomy club, she shines like a firefly among all these dark moths. She tried to get me into one of her dresses, but I didn't like the feel of the night, wanted to know I could run away if I had to, or fight. So I'm wearing the same clothes as always, dark jeans and my favorite disintegrating Siouxsie shirt, boots for kicking. I did let Aurora outline my eyes, mess up my hair. I check myself out in the filthy bathroom mirror. I look mean, which doesn't surprise me, and sexy, which does. Aurora leaves me to go get a drink and I watch her dance through the crowd, touching someone's arm, kissing someone else's cheek.

The air is hot and thick with cigarette smoke and the resinous tang of pot. Red lights are trained on the empty stage and they refract through the haze across a tangle of faces and bodies. I shift from one foot to the other, my skin itchy. Someone elbows me in the back, someone else steps on my foot, and panic surges in my chest—*they're going to crush me,* I think. I can't breathe, and the bodies around me are pressing closer and closer, and I fight the urge to punch into the crowd. "What's the matter?" Aurora asks, coming up behind me and putting one cool hand on my cheek. "You look awful, what happened?" She hands me a drink, something clear and cold, and I gulp it down without asking what it is. Then I see who she's with. It's the skeleton man from her party. He's wearing the same clothes, or some version of the same clothes. His eyes are so dark I can't see where the pupil ends and the iris begins.

"This is Minos," Aurora says. "You remember him? He was at my party? He owns a club in LA, and he works for a record producer." She babbles on. Her voice has the plastic lilt it takes on when she's being charming. The skeleton man watches me with his flat black eyes, as though he can see right through me to that afternoon on the beach with Jack, as though he knows everything I have done and every thought I have ever had. Under that ruthless stare all my feelings seem adolescent and cheap. The stage lights dim and come up again, saving me from having to say anything. Jack comes onstage and the crowd hushes instantly. I can feel the whole club go anxious and expectant around me. Aurora puts her head on my shoulder. "They love him already. Look at that." She pokes me in the ribs. "Love him just like you." I grimace but refuse to rise to her bait.

I thought I had been moved by Jack's music before; that was nothing compared to what happens now. The music washes through the packed room like a flood tide. It's the sound of spring rising out of a cracked and barren earth, gilding branches with new buds and loading vines with heavy blossoms, dusting bees with pollen. It's spring giving way to summer, balmy air smelling of roses, hot skin meeting the cold shock of the ocean, starry nights as warm as kisses. It's the soft touch of lips brushing the hollow of your throat, slow hands on your naked skin. It's as elemental and necessary as the breath in my lungs, but far more beautiful than anything that is real. I open my eyes and look around me and see mouths open, cheeks wet with tears. But the hunger in their eyes terrifies me, their hands reaching for him as though they would tear him to pieces if he were among them. Devour him whole. *No*, I think, *it's too much. It's too much.* But I can't stop it, can't even stem my own desire, how much I want him, how much I want that music in me, too.

When he stops playing he stands for a moment, stilling the quivering strings with the flat of his hand, and then he walks off the stage. The room is as still as a cathedral for long seconds, and then everyone around me lets out their breath at the same time, and the madness leaves their eyes and they shake their heads as though to clear away a spell. Someone begins to clap, slow and uncertain, and then someone else joins in, and then the whole room roars, throats open wide, cheering and stomping their feet. I look over at Aurora. Minos is standing behind her, his arms around her waist, and she is leaning into him with her mouth open. He catches my look and smiles at me, a death's-head grin with no joy in it.

It is a long time before the cheering dies down, and a long time after that before the next band begins carrying their drum kit and amps onto the stage, shoulders hunched as though they are embarrassed. The band launches into its first song and the chords jangle harsh and wrong. They falter and stop, start over again. I've seen them before and they were good, better than good, but there's no way anyone mortal can follow Jack. The singer, a girl with long dark hair and a baby face, seems near tears. Aurora is drinking one clear drink after another. "Let's go," I say to her, and she shakes her head.

"I'm having fun."

"This stopped being fun."

"You don't even try to have fun." She pouts at me. I know Aurora drunk by heart. I don't even need to see the flush in her cheeks or hear the challenge in her voice. Minos lurks behind her, bone-thin but somehow taking up too much space. I don't like him, don't want to talk to him, don't want to watch Aurora flirt with him, giggling, like a rabbit teasing a wolf. He could eat her whole. He looks at me over her shoulder and smiles again. It's not friendly.

"I'm going to find Jack." I push past them before she can say anything else. I cut my way through the crowd to the door that leads backstage, wait until no one is looking and duck through it into the dingy and badly lit corridor.

Jack is in the green room, alone, sitting on a decrepit velour couch that looks like it's been abused by musicians for longer than I've been alive. His guitar is next to him and his head is in his hands. I feel suddenly foolish, duck my head in embarrassment. But he looks up at me with such naked joy that I have to look away. I cross the room and before I even reach the couch he's on his feet, leaning toward me, his mouth meeting mine.

"They want so much," he says into my hair. "Every time I play for more people, they want more of me, and I feel so empty when I'm done. But it's the only thing I know how to do. It's the only thing I'm good at."

"You can learn other things."

"It's the only thing that makes me feel alive." He is holding my wrists now, so tightly it hurts. "Do you want to get out of here?"

"Let's go."

He lives in a one-story cottage caught between two larger buildings. A jungle of front garden hides it from the street: huge, glorious dahlias luminous in the moonlight; heady-scented wild roses; broad-leaved and tall green plants I do not recognize. Cass would know their names. The ground is carpeted with mint, and a riot of jasmine obscures the front porch. I stop to look at the flowers. "I've never seen dahlias this big."

"I play for them," he says. "I think they like it." He unlocks the door and I follow him inside.

The house is a single open room, with a small kitchen in one corner and big windows that look out on another, even junglier garden in back. There's a mattress under one of the windows with a book-stuffed shelf beside it, a cheap card table and two chairs, a soft rich rug, a dresser, a single lamp in one corner. A record player sits beside a wooden crate full of records. There's nothing on the walls except for a print of Henri Rousseau's *The Sleeping Gypsy* tacked up over the bed. I've always loved that painting: the reclining figure stretched out on desert sand underneath a night-blued sky. Multicolored coat, striped blanket, lute. The moon is full, edging a range of mountains in silver. A lion stands over the sleeping figure, one yellow eye staring. Not at the sleeper, but at me. No one in the world knows where I am except Jack. I cross the room and squat next to the bookshelf. Mostly classics: Ovid's *Metamorphoses, The Odyssey*, Keats, Shakespeare. A copy of *The Inferno* illustrated by Gustave Doré. Art books: Lucian Freud, Kiki Smith. "Schiele," I say, "you like him?"

"I love him."

"So do I. You like Rousseau, too?"

He touches the picture. "Did you know he never left France in his entire life? He was a tax collector who painted taxidermied animals and invented a jungle out of the exhibits at the Jardin des Plantes in Paris. He painted people like me without ever having met a black person." He stops and I wait for him to say something else. "It's a reminder," he says. "For me. Of what people see."

"Oh. I never thought about it that way before."

"Well," he says. "You're white."

"Oh," I say again.

He puts on a Nina Simone record, sits on the bed. "Come here," he says gently, and I move up from the floor so that I'm sitting next to him on the mattress. My heart is beating so hard I think he must be able to hear it. Nina Simone's low rich voice seals us in. "What do you paint?" he asks. "Surely not lions." He puts a hand on my back, his thumb gently rubbing the knot of bone where my neck meets my spine.

"People, mostly. Sometimes places. Sometimes things that aren't real."

"Would you paint me?"

"I can't."

"Try."

I hook my bag toward me with my foot, get out the jar of India ink and the soft brushes I carry with me everywhere. I get up, drag over one of his chairs, sit in it facing him, prop my sketchbook on my knees. I look at him for a long time, trying to see him as a series of lines, trying to see the shape underneath his skin, a language of his bones and his body that I can translate into marks on paper. The white page leers at me, mocking. I fidget, chew my brush. Then I have an idea.

"Take off your shirt," I say, "and lie down." He raises an eyebrow. "Not like that." I can feel heat rising to my cheeks, and I turn my head away. "Just do it." I hear the rustle of him moving around and don't look again until he is still. The lamplight gilds the smooth muscles of his back and arms, his long and beautifully shaped hands. He's turned his face away from me, and his hair coils across the pillow. I set down the sketchbook, put my brush between my teeth, and uncap the bottle of ink. "Keep still," I say into his ear, and then I go to work.

I draw a flight of shorebirds winging their way up his spine and a cluster of sea urchins spiking across his shoulder. I draw an osprey, stalled in midair with its wings crooked, in that still moment before it begins its dive. I draw waves rising between his ribs. I draw fish winking silver through the depths, kelp winding around them in thick glossy coils. I thought I knew my own desire, until the wind changed and a storm blew in and remade the sky, dredged mystery from the deep. *I put a spell on you,* Nina Simone croons. His back rises and falls as he breathes, and it is all I can do to keep myself from dipping my head and licking his skin. When the record ends I get up and turn it over. Nina Simone sings about sorrow and love, and the gold of her voice fills the air around us. When I am done I set the brush aside and put one hand over what I've drawn, fingers spread, not touching. Rousseau's lion watches over us, wide-eyed, solemn. The room is very still. I blow on his skin to dry the last of the ink and he shivers, catches my wrist. "Is it good?"

"It's beautiful," I say.

"Show me," he says.

"Do you have a mirror?"

"Not like that," he says. "With your hands."

꧁

You think that the world we live in is ordinary. We make noise and static to fill the empty spaces where ghosts live. We let other people grow our food, bleach our clothes. We seal ourselves in, clean the dirt from our skins, eat of animals whose blood does not stain our hands. We long ago left the ways of our ancestors, oracles and blood sacrifice, traffic with the spirit world, listening for the voices out of stones and trees. But maybe sometimes you have felt the uncanny, alone at night in a dark wood, or waiting by the edge of the ocean for the tide to come in. We have paved over the ancient world, but that does not mean we have erased it.

Once upon a time, girls who were too beautiful or too skilled were changed into other things by angry gods and their wives. A cow, a flower, a spider, a fog. Maybe you boasted too loudly of sleeping with a goddess's husband. Maybe you talked too much about your own talents. Maybe you were born dumb and pretty, and the wrong people fell in love with you, chased you across fields and mountains and oceans until you cried mercy and a god took pity on you, switched your body to a heaving sea of clouds. Maybe you stayed in one place for too long, pining for someone who wasn't yours, and your toes grew roots into the earth and your skin toughened into bark. Maybe you told the world how beautiful your children were, and the gods cut them down in front of you to punish you for your loose tongue, and you were so overcome with grief your body turned to stone.

You know as well as I do that those things don't happen anymore. Girls stay girls, no matter how pretty they are. No matter who lusts after them. But in this time, like in any time, love is a dangerous game.

Who among us has not wanted to be transformed? I had lived all my life surrounded by extraordinary people, and some nights I would fall asleep wishing to wake up worthy of them. Not a painter, but an artist, someone who could capture life in a single perfect line, render the movement of light on water with the stroke of a brush. But the lesson in stories is always that metamorphosis comes with a price. Think of Midas, who asked for the power to turn the world around him into gold, only to sit alone in his palace full of riches, meat and wine turning to metal in his mouth. Think of Icarus, builder of wings, who flew too close to the sun and plummeted in one last fall. Think of Aurora's father, who woke up one morning with his songs playing on every radio in the world. He was never happy again after that, and now he's dead. The old gods do not give kindly; what delights them most is taking away.

Both of them, Jack and Aurora, burned like stars, and light like that draws things that are better left alone in the dark.

⸎

When I let myself into the apartment the next morning I know right away that I am in trouble. Aurora is sitting next to Cass on the couch, her knees drawn up to her chin. Cass is holding a mug of coffee. "Where the *hell* were you," she says, her voice tight.

"I thought you were *dead!*" Aurora cries. She's still wearing her slip, her barrettes askew. There's a blanket around her shoulders. They must have spent the night on the couch.

"You could have at least called," Cass says.

"There wasn't a phone," I say.

"You were with *him*," Aurora says. "You left me at the club and didn't tell me where you went and I came here at three in the morning and told Cass I couldn't find you. We almost called the cops, and all you can say is that there wasn't a *phone*?" Cass puts her hand on Aurora's shoulder.

"Aurora, sweetheart, why don't you go sleep, and I'll deal with this." Without looking at me, Aurora runs into my room and slams the door behind her. "Come into the kitchen," Cass says. I follow her, sit in my favorite chair as she gets down her jars, measures out herbs, puts water on the stove to boil. The silence is like a third person in the room.

"Don't you ever do that to me again," she says at last. "I don't ask a lot of you, and I know you—" her voice breaks. "I know you grew up fast. But I'm still your mother, and you live in my house, and if anything happened to you I don't know how I would keep going. Do you understand?"

"Yes." She sets a mug in front of me. I drink my tea in chastened silence. Nettles and oat straw. She's stopped being mad. If she were still mad she'd have given me burdock or something worse.

"Do I need to give you the safe-sex talk again?"

"*Mom*. He didn't give me a lobotomy."

She shakes her head. "Go to bed," she says, "before I kill you myself."

I think Aurora is fast asleep but when I slide under the covers she puts an arm around me. "I'm still mad at you," she murmurs.

"You were with that horrible man."

"He isn't horrible. He's nice."

"How old is that guy?"

She yawns. "Don't be bourgeois. And you're not off the hook." She closes her eyes and burrows closer to me. I hug her close and we fall into a dreamless sleep.

I wake up hours later. The long afternoon is slipping into twilight. I can hear Aurora in the kitchen, talking to Cass. I sit up, run my fingers through my choppy hair, look at my familiar walls covered in drawings and photo-booth strips of me and Aurora, me and Cass, an ancient one of Cass and Maia with their hair spiked and padlocked chains around their necks, flipping off the camera and kissing in the final frame.

When we first moved into the apartment, Cass let me paint one wall of my room a matte cream and draw on it. Over the years, Aurora and I mapped out our own kingdom, its outlines becoming more legible as my drawing skills improved. We'd started at the very center of the wall, a few feet off the floor. We'd been too small to reach any higher. We drew a village of lopsided houses with stick-figure people holding the leashes of stick-figure dogs. As the drawing spread outward, we added mountain ranges and forests, a sea dotted with tall ships, a solitary dragon undulating overhead. We've never outgrown it. We'll get stoned on a sleepy, rainy afternoon and go to work. When Cass was teaching me to read tarot I drew the Queen of Wands with her cat, Strength and her lion, the Empress reclining on her throne. When Aurora first started sleeping with rockers, she added a slew of long-haired boys. Now, we draw people we know: Raoul and Oscar Wilde, Maia, Cass. We've never thought to add ourselves.

I root through my dresser for a clean pair of cutoffs and a T-shirt, carry them into the bathroom with me, and turn on the shower. Ink runs off my skin, pooling in the bottom of the shower, reminding me of the night before and turning my legs shaky with desire. *I am not this kind of girl,*

I think, trying to be fierce with myself. I am not the kind of girl who ditches her best friend and runs out into the night with a stranger and kisses him until dawn. I am not some lovesick dupe. I am not at the mercy of my new, most favorite vice. I am *not*. I scrub until all traces of the ink are gone and the shower's out of hot water.

Cass and Aurora are still in the kitchen, stir-frying vegetables. A pot of brown rice simmers on the stove. Hippie dinner. I sigh. Some days, like this one, I wish Cass was not a witch so that we could have steak. After we eat, Aurora follows me into my room and rummages through my records, and I know I'm forgiven. She sprawls across my bed with an old issue of *Magnet* and I take out my sketchbook to draw her. We're quiet for a while, Aurora turning pages and humming, me laboring over each line, trying for fluid grace and failing miserably. "I have something for you both," Cass says from the door.

"Presents!" Aurora says happily. "I love presents!" She rolls over, sits up.

"Hey," I say. "Now I'll never finish this." Getting Aurora to hold still long enough for me to draw her is a futile endeavor, but that never stops me from trying. Cass hands us each a bundle wrapped in silk. I unfold the cloth to find a little leather bag on a leather string. She's given Aurora the same thing.

"What's in here?" Aurora says, tugging at the bag's knotted drawstrings.

"Don't," Cass says sharply. "Don't open them. They're bound."

"I know it's bound," Aurora says. "I want to see what's inside."

"Not bound like that," I say. I take Cass's witchiness more seriously than Aurora does, although nowhere near as seriously as Cass does herself. "They're amulets. Thanks, Mom."

"Amulets for what?" Aurora leaves off picking at the strings, but she's still eyeing the bag like she thinks it's full of secret treasures and wants to tear it apart.

"Protection," Cass says. "Safe travels through dark places." Her voice is even. A chill runs through me, and for a moment the room is very still. Aurora stares at Cass. I can see the challenge in the set of her chin. The leather bag is warm in my hand, warmer than the heat of my skin.

"I don't need amulets," Aurora says. They are watching each other like cats raising hackles, growls starting in the backs of their throats. I look from Cass to Aurora and back again. Whatever is happening here, it definitely bypassed go and went straight to really fucking weird without collecting two hundred dollars.

"Hey," I say, but they ignore me. Cass blinks first and Aurora looks away, the corner of her mouth curving up in a malicious smile. "Hey," I repeat. Cass shakes her head as if she's walked into a spiderweb.

"I can only help you if you let me."

"I don't need anyone's help." Aurora hands her amulet back to Cass. "Thanks, though," she says in a normal voice, and some of the tension seeps out of the room.

"You'll wear it," Cass says to me.

"Sure." She looks at me. *Okay.* I loop the leather over my head. The bag settles between my breasts. It's heavier than it felt in my hand.

"Don't take that off," she says. "Good night."

"'Night," Aurora says to her retreating back. "God," she yawns when Cass closes the door behind her. "Your mom is such a fucking weirdo."

"Tell me about it," I agree, touching the leather bag.

"I should go."

"Spend the night."

"Nah." She looks almost furtive. "I have to be somewhere."

"Where?"

"It's nothing."

"Aurora."

"No, really. Just this dumb thing."

"You want me to come?"

"You would hate it," she says.

"I'll still come."

"I know." She smiles. "You're the best. I'll spare you."

"Okay," I say. "Have fun." After she goes I sit on my bed, staring at nothing. We've always had secrets, me and her. But we've never had secrets we didn't share.

Aurora calls me late the next morning, talking nonstop as soon as I pick up the receiver. "What are you doing? Go to the window. Go to the window right now." Dutifully, I carry the phone across the room.

"And?"

"And look outside. Look! Outside!" I peer down the street.

"I'm looking?"

"Tell me that is not the most magnificent motherfucking morning you have ever seen in your natural life, sweet child of mine. We are going out into it, you and I. Call Jack."

"Jack doesn't have a phone."

"Then send him a missive of the heart. We are coming to fetch him. He's going to busk for us."

"I don't—"

"Perfect, I'll be there in ten."

I'm still laughing when she pulls up outside my window, honking furiously. I grab my backpack and take the stairs two at a time. "What are you wearing," she says.

"Clothes."

"God grant me the serenity to accept the disastrous fashion choices of my best friend in all the world, who elects to garb herself in rags even when being transported by her faithful chauffeur to the abode of her beloved, possibly the foxiest man in the entire—"

"He is not my beloved. Lord. What's wrong with my clothes?"

Aurora snorts and takes a corner so fast I nearly go through the open window. "Seatbelts are recommended," she says.

Aurora leaps up Jack's steps and pounds briskly on his front door. He opens it, blinking sleepy-eyed at the morning sun. "Come on!" she yells. "Get your guitar! Come on!" She's on the verge of jumping up and down. Jack looks at me over her shoulder.

"It's like saying no to a tornado," I tell him.

"I see," Jack says. Obediently, he fetches his guitar from next to his bed, puts it in Aurora's trunk, gets in the back-seat.

"We're going to the canal!" Aurora says, gleeful as a toddler. "You can busk and we'll pass a hat around. And then we'll make garlands out of flowers and put them on your head. And everyone will love us and you'll be famous."

"I think the steps to fame are typically more complex," Jack says, but he's grinning.

"Nope," says Aurora. "Stick with me. I'll make you a star."

The grassy parkland along the canal is packed with people. It's a farmers' market day. Hippies tote babies and trail dogs on hemp ropes, and wholesome-looking types are weighed down with cloth bags overflowing with greens. Cass's idea of heaven. If I had the power, I'd send the lot of them straight to hell. Aurora buys a still-warm loaf of bread and some goat cheese and shoves chunks of bread in her mouth as she directs us to a clear spot next to the water. Jack takes out his guitar, tunes it. No one pays much attention. "Play a happy song," Aurora says through a mouthful of cheese.

"The happy songs are never the good ones," Jack says.

"Fine then," she says. "Play something that will devastate us all."

Jack winks at her. When he starts to sing his voice is a surprise: low and rough with the raspy longing of a much older man, weighted with decades of hard living and cruel twists of fate. A bourbon-thick smoker's voice, a voice of old sorrows and older wants. *"I went to the crossroads, fell down on my knees,"* he sings, the chords under his fingers sinuous and sorrowful. I tilt my head back, let the impossible yearning fill me with a hunger I never knew I had. *"Standin' at the crossroad, baby, risin' sun goin' down."* It's as though the pain in his voice strips him naked in front of us, lets us see into the life he had led before we met him.

Lonely nights and cold beds, hungry enough to eat your own shoes, sleeping in ditches and hitching rides to a place you know won't be better. A despair so deep it's like an animal living inside you, a thing you can call by name. Note after shimmering note, suffering spun into a net of music. All around us, people fall silent, turn toward him. Even the birds in the trees still their trilling calls, crickets hushing where they chirp in the grass. Barking dogs sink to their haunches, lay their heads across their paws, fetches forgotten. Aurora takes my hand. When he finishes there is no sound other than the movement of the wind in the trees all around us. Jack bows his head, his braids obscuring his face.

"Jesus," Aurora says. I've never seen her so close to speechless. "You really are the real deal."

He smiles at us from behind the tangle of his braids. "I know."

Jack plays for us until the shadows are long in the grass. Nothing like that first song: lighter things, melodies that move hopping around us like bumblebees, lazy silly songs that make me think of cats in patches of sun, or pedaling downhill with the wind in my face and the world singing all around me. People come forward and drop dollar bills in his guitar case, sheepish, as though they know what they should be offering is something far more precious. A little boy brings him flowers, and Jack lets him put them in the frets of his guitar. Aurora smokes, stretches out in the sun, runs her fingers through her long hair.

At last Jack sets the guitar aside. His case is full of bills, not all of them singles. Other things, too: glass beads, a cheap ring, a packet of incense, a playing card. When I look over at Aurora she is watching me watch Jack, her face serious, her eyes far away.

"We should go get something to eat," I say. Jack tugs idly at the fraying hem of my jeans.

"No," Aurora says. "I mean, you go ahead. I'm not hungry."

Aurora is never not hungry. Aurora would eat veal while watching calves go to slaughter, demanding more condiments. "I'll drop you off somewhere," she adds.

"Can I come over?" Jack asks. I can't stop the stupid smile that spreads across my face.

"Okay," I say. Aurora chews on her hair.

"Fine, then," she says. "Come on." Without waiting for us she hops to her feet, scampers toward her car. Jack puts his guitar back in its case, tucks away his booty.

"That was really fun," I say in the car. Aurora is uncharacteristically quiet. Jack's staring out the window, not paying attention. My words drop into the silence and hang there. When Aurora stops in front of my building, she clears her throat.

"I'm going to a show later," she says. "If you want to come."

"I'm okay," Jack says. "Thanks."

"I guess not," I say.

"Sure," she says. "I'll see you tomorrow."

Cass is out, and the apartment is dark. Jack paces each room as I turn the lights on. I'm anxious, now that he's in my house for the first time. Now that he can see our shabby rugs and derelict furniture. My room isn't clean. I try to remember the last time I washed my sheets. He looks for a long time at Aurora's and my kingdom. I stand in the middle of the floor, watching him, wanting to turn around in embarrassed circles. Something. Anything. I am way too young. He is realizing I am way too young. I am an idiot. Idiot idiot idiot. Id. I. Ot.

"This is really good," he says.

"What?"

"This." He points to some of the more recent additions: Raoul in his vampire clothes, offering up a handful of apricots. A house I drew one sleepless night, with a neat garden and a hobbity round door. A mountain range.

"Oh. Aurora drew some of it, too." I point out where we started. "When we were kids we thought if we got good enough we could climb in."

"You wanted to?"

"It wasn't always so great at home."

"Yeah," he says. "I know all about that one. Do you have anything else?"

"My sketchbook. But you can't see that. Some other stuff that's stupid. Do you want to see Aurora's birthday present?"

Aurora's birthday is next month, and for weeks I've been painting her a banner. I put her at the center, in one of her white dresses with her long hair streaming in elaborate curlicues that turn into twisting, sinuous vines. I surrounded her with jewel-feathered tropical birds that gleam through the foliage. The feathers are taking me forever. So many tiny lines. Roses explode at the corners, giving way to a border of orchids and lilies. Behind her, a sunset colors the sky pink. The whole thing is like Maxfield Parrish on ecstasy. I had to restrain myself from adding a unicorn.

"Wow," Jack says, but I can't tell if he's impressed or horrified.

"It's supposed to be campy," I say quickly.

"It's not at all. It's beautiful. There's so much love in every line." He outlines the curl of a vine with one finger without touching the canvas.

"She's my whole life."

"That can be dangerous," he says.

"Not if you really love someone."

"Especially if you really love someone." He turns back to the banner. I don't know whether to touch him. Don't even know what game we're playing. Like when I was a kid on the playground, every day the other kids knowing by some secret code what clothes to wear, what things to say, me always getting it wrong, not even realizing there were rules.

"I don't know how to talk to you," I blurt. He looks at me in surprise. "You're a lot cooler than I am," I say. "You're beautiful. You're the most amazing musician I've ever seen. You're like a—a—I don't know, you're like a real person. I'm—"

"You're a very real person. You're one of the realest people I've ever met."

"I don't know what that means. Are you telling me I'm stupid? Because I'm not stupid."

He laughs so hard he has to put his hands on his knees. I have no idea what I just said that was so funny. "I haven't known you that long, but I can definitely tell you aren't stupid."

"Does that mean I can kiss you?"

"Yes," he says. "That is exactly what it means."

———

Late that night, after Jack's gone home, Aurora calls me from the club. "Babycakes," she says, her voice slurring. "I'm too fucked up. Come get me."

Cass is asleep and I take her keys without asking. Maybe I'll get lucky and she won't notice. The night is lovely and smells of salt, and I roll my window down all the way. If I weren't driving I'd hang my head out like a dog. I want to enjoy the moment. I don't know what I'll find when I get there.

I'm expecting ambulances, sirens, cops, something. But from the outside the club is still. Inside it's noisy and hot and dark. A metal band screeches from the stage. I peer around the room, check the bar, shove my way through the pit. I can't see Aurora anywhere. If she was still walking she could have gone home with someone in the time it took me to drive here. I try not to think about that. There's a line for the women's bathroom, sullen girls with teased hair and too much eyeliner. "I'm looking for my friend," I say to one of them. "Blond hair. Really pretty. Skinny." I have to shout over the noise. She stares at me.

"Some crackhead bitch has been in the bathroom for a long-ass time," she says. I cut past the line and pound on the door.

"Aurora. *Aurora.*" I hear something shatter. "Ah, shit," I mutter, and throw my shoulder against the door.

I'm strong and the latch is cheap and I only have to hit the door twice before I'm through. The mirror over the sink is in splinters, the bathroom floor scattered with broken glass. Aurora's sitting on the toilet, her white dress stained red. "I cut myself," she says. "You came for me."

The metal girls are trying to push past me into the

bathroom. I haul Aurora to her feet and shove them out of the way. One of them cocks her fists at me but falters when she sees my face. I drape Aurora's arm over my shoulders and half-drag, half-carry her outside. She's as light as a bird.

In the empty street in front of the club she puts her bloody hands against the wall and vomits. I check for damage. Her knuckles are a mess, but the cuts look worse than they are. No one's watching us. I take off my sweatshirt, yank my shirt over my head, put my sweatshirt back on. When she's done throwing up I wrap the shirt around her hands to stop the bleeding. "I'll get your shirt dirty," she mumbles.

"Good thing I always wear black." I steer her to the car. It's better than it could have been. She can almost walk on her own. I roll down the window on her side. "Puke outside the car," I tell her, getting into the driver's seat.

"Outside the car," she repeats. "I love you so much."

"I love you, too."

"I'm such a fuckup."

"I know."

"No more speed."

"No more speed."

"I promise."

"Okay," I say.

"Are you mad?"

"I'm not mad."

"You're mad."

"Aurora. I'm not mad."

"You think I'm going to take him."

"I don't think that."

"You do. I would never do that."

"It's not always up to you."

"You are the first thing to me. Always. You."

"You, too."

"You love him more than you love me," she says.

"Aurora. Never."

"You do."

"I don't love anyone more than I love you. I promise."

"You promise?"

"I promise."

"Promise again."

"I promise."

"One more time."

"I promise."

"I love you," she says again. I reach over and put my hand over the wadded-up shirt.

"I'll always come get you," I say. "No matter what."

Jack is teaching me how to play guitar, and it's not going well. We're sitting on his porch, his long legs folded around me, his hands over my hands, the guitar in my lap. The sun's heavy and low in the sky. The smell of his skin is driving me to distraction. "Here," he says, shaping my fingers over the strings. "That's G major. No, no, you have to keep your middle two fingers—" I knock his hand away in a fit of temper. The *whuff* of his breath ruffles my hair.

"I don't like it," I tell him.

"How can you not like it? I showed you two chords."

"I don't like either of them."

He rests his chin on the top of my head. "I should've known the guitar would be too hard for you. You need to pick a beginner's instrument."

"You fucker! It is not too hard!" Immediately I put my hands back on the strings, bite my bottom lip, try to remember where my fingers go. Behind me Jack chuckles.

"Let no one ever tell you that you are anything other than predictable," he says.

"I am not predictable!" But he only laughs harder and kisses the place behind my ear that sends me straight into a desperate swoon. "I am not," I mumble.

"You are."

"Maybe a little."

"A lot."

"You're a dick."

"Mmmm." He takes the guitar away from me and I scoot over. He strums an aimless melody, a carefree traveler strolling by a river, water singing over stones. Leaves turning in the summer air. I can see the flash of a fish jumping, the mercury buzz of a dragonfly moving across the water. The river's so real I can dip my feet in the cool clear water. The breeze he's conjured plays across my skin. Jack's arms are alight with butterflies, their wings moving softly. Caught, as I am, in his spell. He stops, and I can feel the loss of it like a sob rising in my throat. Wherever he took me, I want to go back. He smiles at me, gentle now, puts his arms around me. He takes the tip of my earlobe in his teeth, and I shiver.

"I can't play like you," I whisper. "No one can play like you."

"Play like yourself, then. Want to learn another chord?"

"No. Maybe. Fine."

"You can't wear pants when you play this one," he says, and undoes the top button of my jeans.

Later, he makes me beans and rice and we eat cross-legged on his floor. The sun's set, but it's still warm. Neither of us is wearing much. Jack peels a mango, and I lie back with my head in his lap as he feeds it to me piece by piece. I'm full in a way that's unfathomable, alive in my animal skin. I want to tear off all my clothes and go running through the forest, catch something and rip it to pieces while it's still warm, grow fur and climb trees and howl at the moon. My skin feels as translucent and bruisable as rose petals, my whole body brand new. "Tell me a story about your family," he says.

"I never knew my dad. I don't think my mom did, either. She's a witch." He raises an eyebrow. "Really." I touch the amulet around my neck. I'd stopped Jack earlier when he tried to take it off. "She reads tarot cards for people and makes them amulets and spells. She can do star charts. Horoscopes."

"Are you a witch, too?"

"Not a very good one."

"Can you read tarot?"

"Sure."

"Will you read mine?" I sit up, steal the last piece of mango, and see that he's serious.

"Okay," I say. "Do you have a candle?"

He gets up from the bed and looks through drawers while I flip through his records, pick out a Jeff Buckley album, and put it on. I get my cards out of my bag. I still use the same deck Cass bought me all those years ago. It's so well-used the card edges are bent and peeling, but the images have lost none of their color or sharpness. I keep the deck wrapped in a piece of silk, which I spread out on the floor in front of him. He sits, cross-legged, solemn, and hands me a candle. I light it and set it between us. "Now, shuffle," I say, handing him the deck. "Think about your question."

"Any question?"

"Any question."

He closes his eyes and I watch as he shuffles, the dark coils of his hair framing his still features. He stops shuffling, opens his eyes. "*Hallelujah*," Jeff Buckley sings, "*hallelujah*." It's so strong, this moment, his skin, his mouth, our breath mingling. It's bigger than anything, but so precise. You think you know something about the world, and then everything changes and you are in this place, this time, and the song is so sad and so glorious and so perfect. It doesn't seem possible that one person, one stranger, could take everything you have ever felt and make it into something so true and vivid. *"I used to live alone before I knew you."* I know what is happening to me is naked in my eyes, and Jack smiles at me and reaches forward, puts his palms against my cheeks.

Here is my life, this life I never knew I could have, here is the whole world waiting for me, all the possible things. My future is as big as the wild night, the wine-dark sea. The smell of him, the heat of his palms on my skin, the curve of his mouth, the line of his throat, his dark hair falling around him. The last *hallelujah* and then it's gone and we are two people in a room again, maybe falling in love. Jack takes his hands away and I breathe in deep, let it out.

"Cut the deck," I say, "and lay out three cards."

He moves slow, serious, turns over each card like it has instructions written on the other side. The Fool. The Lovers. Death.

"Death," he says. "That's heavy."

"Not always. This is the past." I point to the Fool. "This"—the Lovers—"is the present. And the third card is the future."

"Death is the future?"

"It doesn't mean literal death. Not usually. The Fool is someone who's a dreamer, who wants big things. You've set out on a journey on a new road. You're about to discover new things. But you can't keep your head in the clouds forever. You have to make the right choice. You're fearless, but also naive."

"How will I know the right choice?"

"That's up to you. The Lovers is—"

"—Kind of obvious?" He smirks at me, and I blush.

"Not like that. I mean, it can be. It's another choice card. It means part of the choice is a temptation. You can pick the thing that is comfortable, or go somewhere that's scary but can take you to what you really want. It can mean falling in love, too." I can't quite look him in the eye.

"And Death?"

"Death is change. It's a trial, but also renewal. It means transformation, new ideas. A new opportunity."

"So I'm making a choice that will change my life."

"That's what the cards are saying."

He's quiet for a long time. "That sounds about right," he says. Here's my heart, beating out a tattoo rhythm. I could take it out and hand it over. But maybe I'm not what he's thinking about at all.

"I didn't know my father, either," he says. I wait, but he doesn't elaborate.

"Did it bother you?"

"I never knew anything else. Did it bother you?"

Aurora and I lived in a world without fathers, but full of men: musicians, our mothers' lovers, our mothers' friends. A father seems so much tamer and less interesting than the pack of wolves who raised us.

"No," I say.

"Did you know Aurora's dad?"

I think of the drummer, asking me the same question the night Aurora took me to that show. A million years ago. I was a different person then. A person without Jack. "Not really," I say. "He wasn't around long enough to count." He's silent, thoughtful.

"Do you think it makes a difference?"

"Having a dad? I don't know. Do you?" Raoul has a dad, but he never talks about him. Tracy, the normal girl whose house I used to go to, had a dad. A dad like in a movie, who came home in the evenings in a suit he changed out of. Raoul seems happy. I don't know if Tracy was. Jack tilts his head, thinking.

"It must. But then we would be different people." I wait for him to say something else, but he's done.

I know Jack's voice, and his body. I know his music. I know the way he looks at me, and I know how to make him laugh. I know the books he likes and that he doesn't drink and that he is old enough for me to be a lot younger. I know about the restaurant where he works and the crazy waitress who comes in every night shaking from too much speed and the cook who drops fifty-dollar steaks on the floor before he puts them on the plate when he doesn't like the customers. But about Jack's life before he came here, I barely know anything at all. It's like he began when I met him and before that he didn't exist. How much do you need to know to love someone? I used to think you had to know them inside and out, the way I know Aurora; that you had to know every story that went into them, every place they had been. But it turns out love is easier, and infinitely more complicated. It turns out I don't know much.

Jack blows out the candle. The cards scatter beneath us like leaves. He runs his hands along my bare thighs, slides a thumb under the elastic of my underwear. Where he kisses me, my skin turns to fire. We do not talk about fathers after that.

AUGUST

The three of us are in my room. Jack is sprawled on the floor, long legs everywhere, too big for the small space. I'm curled up in a corner, drawing Aurora. She's sitting on my bed, smoking, with her knees drawn up to her chin. Long bony arms, long fingers, beautiful bird-sharp face. The cuts on her knuckles have healed to faint red lines. You wouldn't think they'd both be so hard for me to draw, considering how much I look at them. We're planning her birthday party. Our made-up world is animated on the opposite wall, the evening light playing tricks. The dragon flies over a choppy sea. Aurora reaches over and stubs out the cigarette in a candle. "What's for dinner?" she says, yawning.

"Cass said there was stuff for stir-fry." I put down my sketchbook. "Story of my life." Cass is out doing a reading for a client, told us to eat without her. Cass hates Jack with an intensity that is as palpable as it is irrational, but she tolerates his presence in the house.

"You poor deprived thing. I'll buy you takeout." Aurora waves a hand over my protest. "It's a salary. I'm putting you to work. We have to figure out the guest list and the decorations and the menu and the bands. And what caterer to use. And how much food we should get. And what we're going to wear. And we should design the invitations if we want to get them printed. Don't you think we should have them printed? I think that would be extra classy. Printed invitations."

"Aurora, your birthday is in a week and a half."

"Then we'll have to plan efficiently."

We order a feast from my favorite Chinese restaurant and eat it in the kitchen. Mu shoo pork, six kinds of dumplings, noodles slippery with sesame oil and tossed with scallions and prawns. Aurora bosses us around, makes me unearth three sets of almost-matching silverware and put out cloth placemats and napkins. She lights candles, turns out the lamps. In the gentle glow we are even more beautiful. We fill our plates over and over again until Aurora wails aloud and pushes herself away from the table. "I'm going to die," she cries, "if I eat any more." Jack leans forward and steals a prawn off her plate and she smacks the back of his hand with her fork. They smirk at each other, the air hopping with electricity. I look away. "I want you to play at my party," she says.

"I'd be honored." The warm light falls across his dark skin, his shoulders, the sharply defined muscles of his forearms that flex and tense as he gathers up the plates and carries them to the sink. I imagine the two of them together, her white hair tangled with his black, their long limbs entwined. They belong with each other more than I belong with either one of them. The thought creeps in like poison from a sting. I shove back my chair and get up, measure milk and honey and herbs into three mugs. When the tea is ready we take it into the living room. I put on New Order and Jack sits close to me on the battered couch. Aurora sits on the floor with a pen and a page torn out of one of my sketchbooks, going on about decorations and cocktails and the different kinds of food she should order, and should there be a costume theme—"Masks," Jack says, his breath warm against my ear. Aurora likes that and writes it down.

"Masks," she repeats, tapping the pen against her lower lip. Jack's hands are on my belly, fingers winnowing under the waistband of my jeans. I want to throw Aurora out of the room and arch my hips to meet them. I close my eyes. "I wonder if we could get hummingbirds somewhere," Aurora says. "Wouldn't that be cool? A flock of hummingbirds?" If anyone could get a flock of hummingbirds for her birthday party, it would be Aurora.

Later, in my room, after Aurora goes home, he unbuttons my jeans and tugs them off my hips, pulls my shirt over my head as gently as if he is undressing a child. Touches the amulet but leaves it there. "Which one of us do you like best?" I ask, and he hushes me.

"You silly thing. How could you even ask me that?" He kisses his way down my throat, pausing in the hollow at the base of my neck. *What is happening to me?*

"I love you," I say, but so soft I don't know if he hears me, and I don't want to say it again in case he did. His skin tastes of honey. He whispers my name, over and over, and when I begin to cry he does not ask why, only kisses the salt tracks the tears leave on my skin until I fall asleep in the circle of his arms.

When I wake up my bed is empty and the room is cool. I draw aside the curtain and look out. The patch of sky I can see is as black and starless as obsidian.

The skeleton man is where I know he will be, a shadow darker than shadow. He raises one bony hand to me in a salute, and I know, although I cannot see his face, that he is laughing.

"You are such a fucking goner," Aurora says at the beach the next day. She's coating her limbs with baby oil, running her hands up and down her legs carelessly while all around us people try not to watch and fail. "You'll never get a tan if you don't take your shirt off," she adds.

"I am not and I'm fine," I snap, hugging my knees and glaring.

"Oh my god, *look* at you!"

"I am *fine*."

"You're a pasty little bitch and you're *in love*."

I look around me for something to throw at her head but we didn't bring anything from the car except towels and Aurora's giant bag. She sees me looking, growls. She tackles me, limbs flying, knocking me back onto my towel. I get a mouthful of her hair and a baby-oiled elbow to the jaw. I'm stronger than she is and we both know it, but I'm scared of hurting her and so I yield without a fight. She straddles me, one eyebrow raised, blows hair out of her face like a gangster puffing a cigar. Behind her the sky is an impossible blue. "Uncle!" she barks.

"You won," I point out. "You're not supposed to say uncle."

"*You* say uncle."

"Aunt. Mom. Brother."

"Say you're in love!"

"Second cousin once removed."

"Look at me rolling my eyes. I am rolling my eyes so hard my face might break. At least take your shirt off so I don't look like a giant slut sitting over here by myself, practically naked." She is shouting by "practically naked." I turn my head and catch a batch of frat boys gaping openly.

"We are definitely fulfilling some kind of girls-gone-wild fantasy happening over there right now."

"Stay frosty, motherfuckers!" she bellows at the frat boys, and then she kisses me. Familiar Aurora smell, vanilla and cigarettes; warm skin; soft mouth. Salt breeze on my bare legs, sound of boats creaking in the harbor. She breaks away. "Come on, take off your shirt," she says again, arranging herself on her towel. "For me. Tell yourself, 'Here is a tiny sacrifice I, repressed and angry as I am, am still capable of making for my very best friend in all the world.'"

"Why am I making this sacrifice again?" I obey, trying not to think about the folds of my belly next to the flawless length of her.

"So I'm not alone. You know I hate to be alone. Are you seriously still wearing that stupid thing Cass gave you?" I look over at her, but her face is turned away.

"Aurora. Remember, we covered this. There is no one I love more than you."

"I was joking." She wasn't, though, and I know it, and she knows I know it. "You didn't answer my question."

"I don't know. Maybe it is stupid. It makes Cass feel better."

"Huh." Aurora sits up, finds a plastic soda bottle in her bag, and offers it to me, smiling brightly now. "Dr Pepper?"

"That's not Dr Pepper, Aurora."

"How can you tell?"

"Dr Pepper isn't clear."

"Oh, nonsense." She uncaps the bottle and takes a swig, makes a face. "It is way too early for vodka, you're right. I'll wait an hour." She looks at an imaginary watch, tick-tocks her head at the imaginary second hand, takes another drink, stretches out on her towel. "Much better. What are you doing tonight?"

"What am I ever doing tonight? Hanging out with you."

"Then you're going to a party."

"Oh boy. Sounds great."

"You're a turd. A bratty turd. Come on, it's friends of Minos's. It'll be fun."

"Minos has friends?"

"Minos has lots of friends. Minos has very important friends. Can I ask you something really emo?"

"Shoot."

"How well do you remember my dad?"

The question is so out of the ordinary for her that I don't even register it for a second, distracted as I am by the thought of Minos: Minos and Aurora, whatever is going on with Minos and Aurora and whether I want to know or should know or should intervene or am powerless to stop it, is Jack coming to the party, do I want Jack to come to the party if it's Minos's party, will Minos steal everyone I care about and make them into creepy skeleton people also, am I insane, is Aurora sleeping with my boyfriend. No way. But if I were my boyfriend I would definitely want to sleep with Aurora, so there is that. Aurora's dad. Is Jack my boyfriend? Probably. Yes. No. Definitely. Aurora's dad. What. "Your dad?" I echo, confused.

"Yeah." Her eyes are closed, her face still. "Do you remember him?"

"Not really. You know that."

"I think I'm forgetting him. Like all the way."

"You were a kid."

"I miss him." She's as emotionless as if she is telling me the rest of the afternoon will be hot.

"Of course you do, Aurora."

"You don't miss *your* dad."

"I don't have a dad."

"You can have my dad."

I don't want Aurora's dad. Or maybe I do. What's worse: croaker or bailer? Does my dad even know I exist? That would be classic Cass, cutting and running without even mentioning the pending stork. "I remember him in your garden," I say. I close my eyes, too, trying to project the picture against my lids like an old reel of film playing in a darkened theater. Haze and rain clouds, blurry as Super 8 film, the motions jerky. A sweater. His tangle of bleached hair, his face, his bony arms reaching for me. Green grass in the grey light. Dandelions an electric yellow. But it's so hard to know, now, if what I see is really what I saw or if it's pasted together out of magazine covers and posters in record stores. News footage clips and television specials and that documentary someone made about him that none of us will admit to watching but all of us saw. I know Cass has a copy of it stashed away somewhere; I found it, once, when we were moving. I wonder if anything I remember of him is really mine to share with Aurora or if it's stolen from other people who didn't know him at all. "It's just a picture," I say. "I don't remember what we were doing."

"It's like that for me, too. Frozen moments. Nothing real."

"That's real."

"It's not the same."

"What about Maia? Do you ask her?"

Aurora snorts and doesn't bother to answer. "What are you going to wear tonight?"

"Aurora—"

"I want to talk about something else now."

"Changing the subject every time it hurts is going to catch up with you one of these days."

"Hasn't yet. Want to borrow something? It's a fancy party."

"I'll bring my fancy attitude."

"You cannot wear that repulsive Misfits shirt. I will wail and gnash my teeth."

"I'll wear the 7 Year Bitch one. It only has a couple of holes."

"You are impossible. *Impossible.*"

"I learned from the best," I say, and take her hand.

Aurora doesn't get me in party clothes, but she tantrums at me that night in her room until I let her put makeup on me and festoon me with baubles. "At least look like you are wearing this awful thing on purpose," she says, scowling and tugging on my shirt. She leans in to draw thick black lines around my eyes. She smears the eyeliner with her thumb, checks her handiwork, shakes her head. "More." She goes after me with the pencil again. I duck.

"You always make me look like I got the wrong end of a fistfight."

"Hold still! Jesus, you're like a little kid at the doctor."

I acquiesce to her ministrations, tug on the crucifix of the metal-beaded rosary she's draped around my neck, grimace like a martyr. She mock-slaps me and then pats my cheek. "There, all better. Let's go pick up Jack."

Jack, Jack. I don't like to say his name around her, knowing the way my face lights up when my tongue shapes the word. I can't form the sound without thinking of the taste of him, his hands moving across my body, the way he likes to kiss the place between my breasts and listen there for the metronome of my heart. I'm grateful she's ahead of me, leading the way to her car, so she can't see the flush that starts in my cheeks. I stumble at the first stair and she laughs without turning around. "Fucking goner," she says, "I am never wrong," and not for the first time I think it is not a blessing to be known so well.

Jack hasn't dressed up, either. He's waiting on his porch, his house dark behind him. He puts his guitar in the trunk and folds himself into the backseat gracefully, kisses my cheek. "Hey, lovely," he says into my ear.

"What about me," Aurora says, and he kisses her cheek, too.

"You don't need anyone to tell you you're lovely." There's a hint of reproach in his tone. Aurora puts the car into gear.

"I tried to get her in a dress," she tells him in the rear-view mirror.

"I wouldn't recognize you in a dress," he says to me mildly.

"I wouldn't recognize me in a dress either," I agree.

"Sometimes people put an effort into how they look," Aurora tells the steering wheel.

"I'm not going to put in an effort for Minos," I say. Aurora scowls.

"What is your damage?" she snaps. "He's fun. Jack likes him."

"You don't like him," I say to him.

"I don't think we should have this conversation right now," Jack says, although I don't know which one of us he's telling to stop. "Let's have fun."

"I'm having fun." But Aurora's voice is cold and the air in the car is charged now with some unfamiliar force and all the joy has gone out of the night. I look out the window at the dark empty streets. We're headed downtown. I lean forward to turn up the stereo, but Aurora slaps my hand away. "I mean it," she says, "I want you to stop saying shit like that about him."

"Aurora, I don't think he's a nice guy."

"I don't need a fucking mother."

"I really think we should talk about something else," Jack says.

"I'm not done," Aurora says. "He's my friend, and my friends don't have to be your friends but you don't get to tell me how to live my fucking life, okay?"

"Minos isn't anyone's friend," Jack says quietly. Aurora ignores him.

"Okay?" Aurora is staring at the road, her mouth set.

"Okay," I say, although I'm not sure what I just agreed to. "Okay. I'm sorry."

Aurora stops the car in front of a high-rise downtown, one of those horrible glass and steel monstrosities that's sprung up here and there in the last few years out of the old brick buildings and shabby warehouses. A valet opens her door and she hands him the keys like she's done this all her life. I wonder if she has. Wonder what she's been up to on the nights I spend with Jack. She doesn't look at me as she gets out of the car. Whatever I did wrong, I am not forgiven. I want to go home. "Hey," I say to her back, "I don't feel great all of a sudden. I might go."

Aurora pretends not to have heard me. Jack's opening his door, stops with one leg outside the car, touches my shoulder. "Please," he says into my ear. "Please come." The valet comes around to my side of the car. He's wearing sunglasses, and there is something about his still face and too-white skin that makes me uneasy. He offers me his hand and I take it. His skin is cold and I drop his hand as soon as he's helped me out of the car, resisting the urge to wipe my palm on my jeans. Aurora's already inside. "Please," Jack repeats. He's as nervous as I am. More nervous.

"What do you know that I don't?" I ask.

"Just come," he says. I sigh and let him lead me inside.

I can't shake my growing dread as the elevator climbs to the top floor. The sleek steel doors open onto an empty hallway, as white-walled and harshly lit as a dentist's office, with a single door at the far end. Aurora skips down the hall. Jack balks, then takes a deep breath and grabs my hand. I give him a reassuring squeeze and he looks down at me. His face is serious and still. "It's a party," I say. "Not an execution." He flinches.

"Not for you," he says. I drop his hand.

"I would really, really like to know what it is you are not telling me."

He shakes his head. "Not now. I need you to understand—" He pauses. "Think of it like an audition."

"Audition for what?" He doesn't answer, turns away from me and walks down the hall, guitar case banging gently against his long legs. "Audition for *what*?" The door shuts behind him with a cool *snick*. "I am going to kill both of you," I mutter to the white walls, and follow them.

Behind the door is the biggest apartment I have ever seen. Apartment is the wrong word. *Penthouse,* I think. *I am in a penthouse.* At first I think the walls are made of glass, but then I see they're a series of enormous windows so cleverly installed that they are nearly seamless. Chandeliers filled with real candles hang from the ceiling. The room is dark. Despite the sweeping expanse of space, it is very hot and very crowded. Throngs of tall pale people, holding wineglasses or thick crystal tumblers, draped in fur and silk despite the summer heat. A silvery-eyed woman with a glossy curtain of dark hair spilling down her naked back. A broad-shouldered man with a fierce, handsome face and terrifying eyes. A group of girls who look more or less my age, heads bowed, whispering to one another. One of them turns to look at me and smiles a cold little smile without any kindness in it. Jack and Aurora are nowhere to be seen.

I shrink back against the door, whacking my elbow on the knob. Pain flares through me, and for a second the room sharpens somehow, like before I was trying to look at everything through a haze of fog and now it's fallen away. But what I'm seeing now isn't real, can't be real—men and women with skulls where their faces should be. A woman wearing a dress that looks like it's made out of deerskin stumbles into me, laughs in my face. Jesus. Not deerskin. Parts of a deer. I can see the head with the tongue lolling, the neck smeared with blood. Her hot breath stinks of something awful, like rotten meat. She laughs again at my expression and dances away. I grind the heels of my palms into my eyes, look again. The pain in my elbow fades to a dull throb, and as it does, the faces around me go ordinary again; unfriendly, maybe, but not inhuman. I touch my shirt where the leather bag Cass gave me rests against my chest. I can feel the reassuring lump of it through the worn fabric. I could turn around and leave, right now, leave this place where I clearly do not belong. *Money,* I think, *these people have money,* but it is more than money that smoothes their skin and gives their eyes an uncanny light, shapes their rich clothes so perfectly against the lines of their bodies. They are gorgeous, but there is the same cruel cast to all of their mouths and they stand too straight, hold their long slender limbs with a grace that is designed to make the observer seem graceless. I feel like a heifer at the racetrack. I catch a flash of white hair and wave, see it move toward me. "There you are!" Aurora yells in my ear. "Come outside! Jack's going to play." She's at home here, the beauty of the people around us no match for the light that shines from her, her lanky body, the luscious curve of her very human mouth. She takes my hand and pulls me through the crowd, leads me to a rooftop balcony that's easily four times the size of the apartment.

Out here the press of bodies is a little less, and I take deep gulps of fresh air. Far below us the city is still and dark. A darker shadow of mountains rings the black water of the sound. I want, more than anything, to be out there instead of here, rolling out my sleeping bag under a clear sky disordered with stars. Both of them with me, faraway and safe. *There is still a chance for us,* I want to say. *We can go. We can walk away from this, from all of it.* But Aurora's eyes are big with delight and she's pressing a glass into my hand, chattering away at me. In her element. So lovely that everyone around us turns toward her, moves closer, brushes up against her as if the magic she has is somehow transferable. I take a sip of what she's given me and the liquor courses through me, fiery as acid.

"Holy shit!" I cough. "What is that?"

"Don't know!" she says. "Crazy stuff, right?" She whoops, throwing her head back, white hair flying. "Come on, I want you to meet someone." I finish the rest of what's in my glass and she finds me another. *In for a penny, in for a pound,* I think, and gulp it down, too. Aurora's hand in mine is cool and light. Whatever I'm drinking scrubs the fear right out of me, sends the edges of everything spinning. Aurora is at home here, Aurora will keep me safe. Aurora would never lead me into harm. I'm seeing things, foolish me, sent aflutter by a few rich people in a fancy room. I've been around rich people before. Rich people are very specific but not particularly harmful. Specifically dressed. Specific in a specific way, like they have weird parties in their clothes. This is profound. I'm going to explain to Aurora about rich people, but my whole body is blooming. Here we are, reckless and young and free as animals. If I jumped off the roof right now I bet anything I'd grow wings and fly. No wonder Aurora wants this. I want it, too, now, want to feel like this forever, want this the way I want sex or music or the feeling of my muscles moving as I run farther and farther into the hills. The warm air buoys me up in the limpid night. My glass is full again and I drink, keep drinking. The air tastes like candy.

Aurora narrows her eyes at me, her mouth moving, saying something, laughing, is it important, probably it's not important, I don't care. The mountains are talking to me, the water singing, all the salt in the ocean calling to the salt in my blood, Aurora, I can feel my heart beating, I mean really feel it. Did I say that out loud, or not, I can't tell, is it important, probably it's not important, I don't care. Did I say that already? It's pretty funny, I'm laughing. She's laughing. The two of us laughing, together, arms around each other, laughing from someplace all the way in the soles of our feet, it's *really funny*. The no-longer sinister faces around me are suffused with a soft glow, rictus grins smoothing out into smiles of real warmth and affection. How could I ever have been afraid of this? I want to find Jack and drag him off into a corner, I want to tell him that I love him, but more importantly I want him *right now*. I want to tell Aurora I was wrong, wrong about everything, how nothing that makes me feel this good could be a bad idea, but she's talking to someone, telling him my name, pushing me forward. A white hand reaching toward me, long pale fingers on my skin. The touch of them burns like someone's thrown me naked into a snowbank.

The man in front of me is impossibly tall and so white he glows with a phosphorescent light of his own against the velvet dark. Eyes the watered-down blue of ice chips, hair as pale as Aurora's falling to his shoulders. Cold bores through me, cold mouth, cold still face. The twin vortices of his merciless eyes, filled with a hideous, intelligent cruelty. All the liquor in the world could not insulate me from the terror of this man, and the luscious haze runs out of me so fast it sets me reeling. His ice-colored gaze pins me where I stand. He takes his hand away, and I half expect to see blistered skin where his fingers touched me. "That's Minos's *boss*," Aurora whispers in my ear. "He's going to make Jack *famous*."

"Delighted," he says. The laughter in his eyes is infinitely more awful than Minos's dead stare. My mouth opens, jaw working, but nothing comes out. I'm saved from having to say anything by Jack's first perfect chord. Aurora tugs me away from the awful man and toward the source of the music. I can feel his stare on my skin even as the crowd closes in around us. I want nothing more than to lie down and let the balm of the drink wash over me again. "Come on," Aurora says. "He needs us." For once she's the strong one. "Come on." Her pupils are so huge they've nearly swallowed her irises whole.

The patio is thick now with people, their conversation unintelligible and raucous, rising all around me like a murder of crows. Aurora holds my hand tight and we stare around us at the sea of strangers. Jack is standing at the very edge of the roof, his head down, his face hidden behind his hair. A fat man in a donkey mask runs laughing in and out of the crowd, followed by the girls I saw before, half-naked now and wreathed in grape leaves. I see a man whose torso ends in goat's legs and another crowned in antlers. *You are drunk,* I tell myself. *You are drunk, you are drunk, you are drunk.*

Jack strikes another chord, and that terrible audience howls aloud with one voice, the unearthly shriek growing louder and louder until I clap my hands over my ears. The music is a huge and terrifying thing that sends flights of dark birds spinning into the night sky. The air is growing hotter, thicker, unbearably stifling. A storm front is rolling in, moving so quickly across the sky that it looks as though someone has spilled a bottle of ink across the stars.

Bodies dance past me, stinking of filth and sulfur. Hands grab at my hair, my arms, tearing at the thin fabric of my shirt. Women whirl by, clawing at one another until blood runs down their shoulders and their naked breasts. Men and things that are not men loom over me, some of them masked and some of them with faces that are worse than masks. A man with the head of a bull. A woman with a swan's wings and a swan's serpentine neck. A woman with a quiver of arrows strapped to her back, cool grey eyes. A swarm of beetles streams over my feet. Still Jack plays, and the mass of bodies twists and seethes. Over it all I hear the groaning rumble of thunder. The sky flashes white, and Jack falters. The dancers freeze in place, teeth bared, smeared in blood and sweat. The air around me is fuzzing like static on a television, cutting to images of the bone-white trees. The noise of the river, the howling dogs. A great black palace rising out of the distance, its edges sharpening. Aurora is no longer at my side, and I look around, frantic, see her leaning into Minos, his fingers a bony cage around her shoulders. Her mouth is slack, her eyes empty. "Aurora!" I scream, but my voice is lost in a crack of thunder, the rising wind. The tall pale man is behind them, watching Jack play and smiling. Cass's amulet feels like a stone around my neck and I fumble at it with my free hand, trying to undo its knots. My palm bumps against the leather bag, and I can hear Cass's firm voice cutting through the chaos around me, clear as if she's right next to me. "Go. Get out of there. Go." *But Aurora. Jack.* "I mean it. Go."

I stumble through the crowd, punching and kicking until the packed mass of bodies parts to let me through. Back to the apartment, the chandeliers dripping wax in searing droplets that land in my hair, on my shoulders. Hands grab at my body, my breasts, my clothes. *Like you're running a marathon. Go. Go. Go.* Head down, battering ram, out, out, out. I reach the door, the knob burning my skin, the door sticking, pulling with all my strength, screaming in terror as the surge of people presses me up against the metal and wood and I think for a second I am going to die here in this awful room—and then with a crack the door springs free of its frame and I'm falling into the hallway, the door slamming shut behind me.

The hall is absolutely silent. I lie panting on the spotless white carpet. There is no hint of what I've left behind on the other side of the door. The walls are lurching around me, and I realize for the first time how drunk I am. I crawl to the elevator on all fours, slap at the down button, roll myself in when the doors open with an ordinary ping. The ride down takes forever. My stomach is roiling, and I wonder what happens if you puke in the elevator to hell. Bad things. I'm using the walls to get to my feet when the elevator stops with a jolt and I fall again out the open doors, landing in an undignified heap at the feet of the valet. "Sorry," I manage. He offers me his hand, and I take it, trying not to flinch at the touch of his clammy palm as he helps me stand. He doesn't say anything. Turns the sunglasses toward me, holds my shoulders until I'm steady. Smiles. There's no way I am imagining it: His teeth are pointed, and I think I see the flicker of a tongue forked like a snake's. *Holy shit.* I back away, trying not to panic. "That's some costume," I whisper. His lips close over the terrible teeth, making the smile somehow even more ghoulish. I stumble past him, out of that awful building, out into the safety of the night.

I walk for a long time before I find a phone. I am drunk and my clothes are torn and I can only imagine what I look like; I caught a glimpse of the smeared mess of my eyeliner in the valet's mirrored sunglasses. Even Cass will never let me out of her sight again if she sees me like this. I dial Raoul's number instead of my own. He answers on the tenth ring, his voice sleepy.

"Hello?"

"I'm in trouble," I whisper.

"Tell me where you are," he says, the sleepiness gone. "And don't go anywhere until I get there."

Raoul rubs my back while I throw up in his toilet, and I am so miserable I don't even feel shame. When I'm done I curl up on the floor of his bathroom and whimper.

"Come on, kiddo," he says. "Let's get you to bed."

"Your bathroom is very clean."

"I like to maintain an appropriate convalescing environment for underage substance abusers at all times." He tugs me to my feet and steers me back to the couch, covers me with a blanket, brings me water. Throwing up has made me feel only marginally better.

"Your apartment won't stop moving. I'm going to die," I wail.

"Eventually," he agrees, "but probably not in the immediate future."

"I *want* to die."

"That's different." He strokes my forehead and the coolness of his touch soothes the throbbing. "You want to tell me about it?"

I tell him. I tell him everything. About the deer dress, the ice-eyed man. The black birds that came out of nothing. Cass's amulet saving me. The valet and his forked tongue. When I'm done, Raoul is silent.

"I was really drunk," I say. "I'm still really drunk."

Raoul nods. "You are very drunk."

"You think I'm making it up."

"No. I don't."

"You don't?"

"I don't." Raoul doesn't know Aurora well, although he's

met her a few times. He's never liked her parties, says he doesn't feel safe. I never knew what he meant until now. "There are different kinds of real," he says. "For now, I think you should get some sleep. And I would like you to promise me you will never drink that much again."

"I will never drink that much again. Will she be okay?"

"Sweetheart, I don't know. Maybe not."

I left her there, I think. *I left her there.* Like Cass. Scorched earth, cut and run. Cass's amulet got me out, but it sure didn't do much for my friends.

"Raoul, what do you do if you fucked up and you don't even know how?"

He kisses my forehead, straightens the blanket. "You'll figure it out. I know you. Now go to sleep. When you wake up I'll make you breakfast."

"When I wake up it will be the middle of the afternoon."

"Breakfast is a state of mind, not an hour."

"I love you, Raoul."

"I know. I love you, too."

"I'm scared."

He takes my hand. "It's always okay to be scared," he says. He holds my hand until I fall asleep.

No hangover in my life has ever compared to the staggering misery that greets me the next day. The light streaming through Raoul's open windows pierces me like a hundred terrible knives. The clank of Raoul's spatula against his frying pan is as loud as a freight train derailing. I moan feebly, shielding my eyes from the sun's blinding assault, and Raoul peers over at me. "How are we feeling?" he asks cheerily.

"Why are you *shouting*," I croak.

"My goodness," he says. "You really did have a lot to drink."

"I am definitely going to die."

"Have some potatoes first. It'll help, I promise." He brings me a plate piled high with greasy breakfast delights. The smell of food nearly sends me running to his bathroom again. Raoul offers me a forkful of potato and chilies. I open my mouth obediently, manage to gum the potatoes into a paste and get them down. He's right; they do make me feel better. "Do you need to call your mom?"

"It's fine. She thinks I'm at Aurora's." Raoul feeds me more fried potatoes until I can sit up, cradling my pounding head in my hands.

"Do you want to call Aurora?"

"What time is it?"

"Not that late. Around one."

I nod without thinking and the pulsating effects of the movement make me groan aloud. Raoul does his best not to laugh at me as he brings me the phone. "Shut up," I say, and dial Aurora's number. To my utter surprise, she answers on the first ring.

"Babycakes! What the hell happened to you last night?"

"I got—" I got what? The raging heebie-jeebies? An invisible burn from Aurora's new buddy? I saw some chick in a steak dress and freaked the fuck out? "I got sort of drunk. Are you okay?"

"Why would I not be okay? I'm great. God, that party was so much fun. I can't believe you left. Jack played for so long, and it was so good and everybody loved him, and Minos loved him, and Minos's boss loved him, and it was seriously like the best thing ever. I almost threw myself off the roof at the end it was so good. You know when something is so good and you think, 'Shit goddamn, girl, that's it, the pinnacle of your life has been achieved and it's all downhill from here'?"

"Are you on meth?"

"What? No. Haven't you ever felt like that? Anyway, come over. I need help decorating and Jack has big news."

There is so much to unpack in that statement that I settle for dealing with the information most relevant to my immediate interests. "Jack's at your house?"

"Where else would he be? Do you need me to pick you up?"

Where else would he be. Right. I make a steering-wheel motion at Raoul. He rolls his eyes and nods. "Raoul can give me a ride."

"Wicked. Come over whenever."

"I guess she's fine," I say to Raoul when I hand the phone back to him. But I can't shake the feeling that something has been set in motion that can no longer be undone. I wish I knew what really happened last night. What I saw and what was because of Minos's sketchball homebrew. I remember the euphoric feeling the drink gave me, that perfect moment of joy. If that's how Aurora feels around him, no wonder she won't shake him loose. I do know what she meant. I'd wanted to jump off the roof, too.

"Are you ambulatory?" Raoul asks, interrupting my reverie. "I have to go to work in a bit, so if you want a ride I should take you now."

"You are a saint," I say. "A saint among mortals."

"The company you've been keeping lately," he says,

"I don't know if you want to be joking about saints and mortals. Come on."

When I let myself in to Aurora's house I hear piano music. I follow the source, expecting to see Jack. But it's Maia at the dust-covered grand piano. Her back is to me and she doesn't hear me come in. Silent, I watch her play.

Her hands move over the keys like liquid, drawing out a tide of swirling notes. I can feel myself sinking into water, some blue country where the light splinters blue-green overhead, and though I can reach for the fragmented rays I can never touch them, lost as I am in the deep. Maia's body sways as though she's possessed, caught in the same heady current that washes us both where it will. The melody sings against a flurry of chords, the strange rhythm carrying us both far out to sea. I have no idea how long she's been playing when she leans back, hands raised. I open my eyes, blinking at the suddenly unfamiliar world of Aurora's house, thinking she is done; but she brings her hands down in a last furious surge, music spilling out in a massive wave, her hands sweeping across the keys and coming to rest at last on a single perfect chord.

I let out my breath in a huge sigh, and Maia jumps, turns to face me. She's out of breath, her cheeks flushed.

"Oh, hi," she says, her expression guilty. "I didn't know you were there."

"That was beautiful," I tell her. "It was like being underwater."

She smiles. "'*Chaque flot est un ondin qui nage dans le courant.*'"

"What?"

"Ravel's *Ondine.* It's about a mermaid who falls in love with a mortal and tries to tempt him to come live with her in her ocean palace. She promises him he'll be a king. When he tells her he's in love with a human woman, she laughs at him and vanishes in a shower of rain."

"That's depressing."

"Not really. She's not human. She doesn't feel things the way human beings do. She likes the idea of the mortal world, but what she's feeling isn't love the way we know it. And if she brings her lover underwater she'll kill him. You can think of it as a happy ending." Maia is the most animated I've ever seen her, emphasizing her points with her hands. "*Ondine* is the first movement. Ravel based the entire piece on a book called *Gaspard de la Nuit,* by the poet Aloysius Bertrand. The whole book deals with night creatures and darkness, the twilight world. Ravel was trying to make a play on Romanticism, but he said later that he thought the piece had gotten the better of him. He became completely obsessed with Bertrand while he was working on the piece. He told a friend that the devil was inspiring him to write the music the same way the devil had inspired Bertrand to write his poetry. '*Boudeuse et dépitée*' is what Bertrand says of the mermaid: peevish and sulky, not heartbroken. None of the creatures from that world understand the way human emotions work. They're all mimicking what they see in us. They can't create things. They can only steal from us. They're forever crossing over to wreak havoc because they're jealous."

Maia's eyes have a feverish gleam, but for once I'm sure she's sober. The lecture is jarring, and I don't like where this conversation is going. Given what's been happening in my life lately, I'm none too thrilled to hear Maia citing the devil as an everyday source of other people's artistic inspiration. "I never knew you played," I say, changing the subject. "You're really good."

Her face goes blank. All the life seems to run out of her as I watch. I don't know what I've said wrong. "I used to be," she says. "Jack and Aurora are upstairs." I take the hint and leave her staring at the piano.

Jack and Aurora are in Aurora's bed watching *Aliens*. They aren't touching, I notice, and then hate myself for noticing. Hicks is showing Ripley how to use the grenade launcher. This scene never fails to send Aurora and me into a frenzy of lust. "Is it normal, do you think," I say, squeezing between them, "to experience actual feelings of loss and anguish over the fact that Hicks is not a real person?" Jack nods solemnly, puts his hand at the small of my back. "I didn't know Maia played the piano," I add.

"She's weird about it," Aurora says, gnawing on a piece of beef jerky. "She won't do it if she knows I'm in the house. Oh my god, *look* at him. Go, Ripley, go."

"Does she play a lot?"

"She was going to be a concert pianist or something."

"She's incredible."

Aurora shrugs. "Fat lot of good it does her. Shut up, this is the good part."

"It's all the good part."

"Shut *up*."

"How are you feeling?" Jack asks me.

"Not my best. How are *you* feeling? That was some show."

"Shhhh," Aurora says, riveted to the screen.

"Aurora, we have both seen this movie at least forty times."

"I'm a little tired," Jack says.

"Did you see anything—" I pause, not even sure of what I'm asking. "Weird? Did you see anything weird?"

"What do you mean, weird?"

"*Shhhhhhhh.*" Aurora smacks me. "For fucking *real.*"

I roll my eyes, lower my voice. "Like, you know, weird."

"I don't notice much when I play."

"You were really drunk," Aurora says to me, not looking away from the screen.

"Not that drunk. Who was that guy you introduced me to?"

"You should ask Jack who that guy was."

I look at Jack. He turns his face away. "What," I say.

"Come outside with me," he says. We leave Aurora, rapt in her bed, and I follow him downstairs and into the jungle of her garden. He finds a less-tangled patch in the shaggy lawn, sheltered from the house by a thicket of blackberries. He lies down in the grass. I stretch out next to him and put my head on his chest.

"You're going to tell me something shitty," I say into his shirt.

"I'm not going to be around for much longer," he says. "They want me to go to Los Angeles. Cut a record. Minos has a club there. I can headline some shows. It's a big deal."

"That's what you were auditioning for."

"More or less."

"What do you mean, more or less? Who was that guy? Minos's boss?"

He puts his arms around me and doesn't answer.

"You saw what I saw," I say.

"I told you, I don't notice much when I play."

"When do you leave?"

"I don't know. Soon. It's not up to me."

"Will you come back?"

"I don't think so."

"Can I come?"

"Oh, you." I wait for him to say something else. *Of course you can come with me. I wouldn't dream of going anywhere without you.*

"What did you promise them?"

His arms tighten around me. "Nothing I'm not willing to give." His voice is steady. The ordinary sun beams overhead in an ordinary sky. Birds chirp, butterflies flutter. I will not fucking cry. If it kills me, I will not cry.

"Does Aurora know?"

"She knows."

"And now I pretend like everything is okay until you leave?"

"You don't have to pretend anything. But I'd like to enjoy the time I have left with you."

"So I pretend." I sit up, furious. "To make it easier for everyone. Why don't you go fuck yourself, Jack."

He reaches for my hand but I pull it away. "You knew what I was when you met me," he says.

"Is this about Aurora?"

"Oh, for fuck's sake." Now he's angry, too. "No, this is not about Aurora."

"Why was it ever me, and not her," I say. He sits up, puts his hands on my knees. This time I don't back away. He looks at me until I have to meet his eyes.

"You're so strong," he says. "The first time I saw you, in that garden, you seemed so sure of yourself. You have this relentlessness, this fury. You say what you think. You're not afraid of anything. You're not like anyone else I know. Do you want me to keep going?"

"Nobody loves the girl who is strong. They love the girl who is beautiful."

"I love you," he says. So low I almost miss it. I will not cry in front of him. I will not. I will not. I will not.

"Not enough." My voice does not waver.

"What if you had to choose? Between art and me? What if you had to go someplace I couldn't follow?"

"I would choose you. I would stay here."

"No," he says gently. "You wouldn't. You're seventeen. Your entire life is in front of you. You're good. But more than that, you're stubborn. You don't take anything for granted. You're so young, and already you understand what it's like to work. You'll love other people. But you would never be able to survive letting go of your art. I can't, either."

"I'm sure Aurora understands." My voice is low and mean and I hate myself even as the words leave my mouth.

"I can tell you the same thing over and over. But it won't do any good if you don't listen to me."

"You want what happened to Aurora's dad? Is that what you fucking want? You want to be so famous it kills you?"

"I'm a lot stronger than Aurora's dad."

"You never knew Aurora's dad."

"I don't have to know Aurora's dad to know I have something he didn't. I'm not going to make the same stupid mistakes he made."

"You're an *asshole*," I snap, balling my hands into fists. I could hit him now without thinking twice. But he doesn't take his hands from my knees, doesn't back down.

"Always ready for a fight," he says, touching my cheek. I flinch and he takes his hand away. "What if someone offered you a trade? Everything you've ever wanted. The whole world. For it to be easy for the first time in your life. No more sleeping on the street. No more playing shitty clubs for six people who are so drunk they have no idea how good you are. No more getting followed home at three in the morning from your shit job washing dishes, getting your ass kicked by bored white boys who don't have the balls to fight you alone. Just music. Just you and the thing you need the most, the only thing that matters."

"Trade for what." *The only thing that matters.* The only thing that matters isn't me. "A trade for *what.*"

He shakes his head. "Let me go. Please. Spend the next few days with me, and then let me go."

I try to swallow past the lump in my throat. "I can't."

"You have to." There is nothing I can say to that, so I don't say anything at all. He kisses my throat, behind my ear, the curve of my shoulder. Skims his palms up the line of my back, fingertips ticking off each vertebra. I let him take off my shirt, unzip my jeans, make a nest of our clothes in the long grass and bring me to him. The air is heavy with the scent of roses, the warm honeyed buzz of a bee. His hands on my skin are cool, his mouth hot. I can hear the earth thrumming beneath us like a pulse.

"I'll take you home," he says later, lazily flicking away an ant making its way up my wrist. Sweat's cooled on my skin. I smell like him. If we don't put our clothes back on, if we lie here in the grass forever, if I don't think about anything, I can make this moment last for the rest of time. But he's already sitting up and buttoning his shirt, his back turned to me. Now that we're not touching he's worse than a stranger. How can someone be so close to you and then so far away in the span of a single movement? Is this a thing that makes sense when you turn into an adult?

"I'll go say goodbye to Aurora." We never did decorate. I go back into the house, still barefoot. Aurora is fast asleep in her bed, clutching the bag of beef jerky. On the screen, Ripley's tucking Newt into her pod. Aliens defeated and everyone safely on their way home through the vastness of space. I turn off the television. Aurora murmurs in her sleep. I stand watching her for a while. All around me the enormous house is still. Everything is on its way toward an end I can't see. Aurora's white hair spills around her, moving with the rise and fall of her breath like a living thing. One strap of her tank top has slipped off her shoulder. "I love you," I say into the silent room. "But I wish you would tell me what the hell is going on." She does not stir.

In the driveway, Jack's straddled his motorcycle. He gives me his helmet and I put it on. I wrap my arms around his waist, remembering the first time we went to the beach together, the first time I touched him, the first time he kissed me. I wonder if he's remembering it, too, or if he's already thinking about what happens next. The part that I'm not invited to. The sun's setting, the sky gone glorious. Let's go for a drive. Let's keep going, out of the city, out west until we run out of land. Let's swim naked in the ocean, phosphorescence streaking behind us like comets' tails, let's shuck oysters on the beach and eat them raw next to a bonfire. Let's build a shack in the woods when winter comes, weather out the long rains with a pile of blankets and Jack's guitar. Let's make a world of our own so strong that no other worlds can intrude on it, no skeleton men, no ambition, no horizon, no fear. No mermaids singing us down to a world we can't survive. I don't say any of it. When Jack stops in front of my house I tug the helmet off, hand it back to him. "You can come in."

"I need to practice." He's looking at the helmet as if it might tell him something important.

"I'll see you later?"

"Later," he agrees, and puts on the helmet without so much as a kiss. Well then. I watch him drive away into the lowering night, knowing that's as close as we'll come to goodbye.

Aurora's birthday is the same night as the full moon. She offers to pick me up, but I bike to her house that afternoon instead, tucking her banner into my backpack after I've rolled it up carefully in butcher paper. I love the long ride to Aurora's, the miles dropping away, the feel of my muscles bunching and releasing on the inclines, the freedom of the downhills. I feel strong and careless and invincible. My shirt is soaked through by the time I reach the elaborate gate that marks Aurora's driveway. This late in the summer, the blackberry vines are weighted with fruit. I hop off my bike and help myself to a handful, wheeling the bike with my other hand as I lap berries out of my palm.

She comes running out to greet me, white hair flying. "You're all sweaty," she says, flinging herself into my arms, wrapping her bare legs around my waist. I laugh and hoist her up, stagger with her across the lawn. "You look terrible." She kisses me. "You're not wearing that to my party, are you?"

"You're in your underwear," I point out.

"I am not in my underwear. I'm wearing a shirt over my underwear." She untangles herself from me.

"Were you going to put clothes on?"

"Oh, eventually. Come help me finish decorating."

Maia's nowhere to be seen. I help Aurora string up paper lanterns in the garden. The caterers show up shortly after I do, shouting orders at each other and carrying folding tables across the lawn. Aurora and I drink gin and tonics on her back porch, watching them mow a swath the size of a dance floor into the tangle of lawn and garland the vine-shrouded portico with lights. "Come on," she says. "We have to get ready."

We fill her enormous bathtub with hot water and lavender-scented oil. I drop my clothes on the marble floor and sink to my ears in steamy, sweet-smelling water. Aurora undresses with her back to me and slinks into the bath, but not before I see the bruises spanning her ribcage. She sees me looking and ducks her head under the water before I can open my mouth.

"Jack's leaving," I say instead when she comes back up.

"I know."

"You knew for how long?"

"Don't be mad at me. It wasn't my story to tell."

"I don't know who you are anymore," I say, helpless. And then I do cry, hot wracking sobs that come from somewhere deep in my gut, and she sloshes forward and puts her arms around me. I cry into her shoulder until we are both a mess of my snot and tears, and she strokes my back and whispers meaningless things in my ear until I calm down and cling to her, hiccupping.

"You know who I am," she says. "I'm the same person."

"You're not the same person." I knot a lock of her hair around my finger. "You knew he was leaving and you didn't tell me. You have all these secrets now. You're sprung on a total monster and I hate him and I hate everyone at that stupid party and I hate—"

She puts her hand over my mouth, gentle, and I take a shuddering breath through her fingers.

"There are things that don't change," she says. "The thing that will never change is how much I love you. Do you know that?"

I shake my head. Yes. No. Yes.

"Don't break my heart," she says. "You know that. Tell me you know that. I will love you until the moon falls out of the sky and we are old women in sensible shoes and our main joy in life is spying on our underage neighbor as he mows the lawn with his shirt off."

I can't help it. I start to laugh. "I can never stay mad at you."

"Because you have nothing to be mad about and because you love me, too. Can you be happy, for me, tonight? For my party? For Jack? Can we wait until tomorrow to be sad?"

That is the story of you, Aurora: You are always waiting until tomorrow to be sad. You're a fairy princess beaming at me, remaking the world in your image. Wiping away everything that hurts. But someday everything that hurts will come back and kill you. Your face, your wide dark eyes, your white hair, the skin I know as well as I know my own. "Okay," I say. "For you, tonight, I will be happy."

"See? It's easier than you thought."

"Aurora?"

"Yeah?"

"Will you stop hanging out with Minos?"

She goes still. "I can't."

"Why?"

"He told me he can take me to see my dad."

"Aurora. Your dad is dead. Your dad's been dead for fifteen years."

"I know that," she says. "But you know Minos isn't like other people."

"I know he's a lot fucking creepier than other people."

"You promised me you'd stop. You promised me now we wouldn't talk about this."

"I'm sorry."

"You're not sorry."

"No. Seriously, Aurora, come on. Your dad—"

"It's easy for you," she interrupts. "You live in a world that's black and white. You're so sure of everything all the time. What's good. What's bad. I've always envied you that, but sometimes it drives me nuts. I'm not like that. Nothing about my life is like that. Not even the color of my skin." I'm crying again, and I don't even know why. She splashes bathwater at me. "Look what you did. Knock it off. We're happy."

"We're happy," I agree. She tosses me the washcloth and I scrub the tears from my face.

"Listen," she says. "There's something else."

"What."

"I might go to LA for a while, too."

"With Jack?"

"With Minos. I mean, yeah, Jack will be there. But I probably won't even see him. Or not very much. I've never been, can you believe that? Minos thought it would be fun."

"You and Jack. You're both—"

"Babycakes. Come on. It's not like that. This is me, okay?"

I know better now than to ask if I can come. "We're happy," I say. It takes all the will I have to keep my voice from shaking. Her smile lights up her whole face.

"I knew you wouldn't care." She flings her arms around me again. I bury my face in her shoulder so this time she can't see me cry.

I start to put my clothes back on after we are done with our bath but Aurora takes them out of my hands. "No," she says. Still naked, she disappears into her walk-in closet. I wait, listening to her mutter and crash around. "Here!" she shouts at last, triumphant, emerging with a handful of glitter and fabric that she thrusts at me. I hold it up, letting its full length hang, and shake my head. It's like something made out of cobwebs—pale, nearly transparent silk, whisper-thin straps and plunging back, strung with glass beads that catch the lamplight and send it flying.

"No way," I say. "This is not even enough fabric to qualify as a garment."

"I wear it," she says, indignant.

"An hour ago you were walking around in your underwear. Pick something else. Anyway, there's no way this will fit me."

"No," she says. "It's my birthday. My present is you in this dress. It's big on me, it'll fit you fine. Take your bra off, you can't wear one with this thing."

I roll my eyes and obey, holding up my arms so that Aurora can put the dress on me. It pours around me like water. It does fit, after all. Silk whispering against my skin. I try not to touch it. Without my jeans, my hoodie, I feel exposed, helpless. Aurora wears these fairy clothes like armor but on me they feel like a trap. She turns me around so that my back is to the mirror and holds up one hand. I wait while she scampers into the bathroom and comes back, wearing a kimono and with her hands full of tubes and compacts. "Sit on the bed," she says, "so I can do your face." I close my eyes as she daubs my skin with creams and powders, feeling the cool swoop of liquid liner across my eyelids, the whisk of a brush dusting color on my cheeks. When she stops I open my eyes again. Her face is inches from mine, her huge dark eyes studying me thoughtfully. Impulsively, I lean forward and kiss her. She smiles against my mouth, puts her hands on either side of my face. She tastes like gin and cigarettes and sugar. "I have to do your hair," she says, her mouth still against mine.

"I love you. Happy birthday."

"I know. Hold still."

When she's done she parades me in front of the mirror. She's mussed my hair in an artful way. The dress clings and sparkles, and I cross my arms over my breasts. "I can't wear this," I say, horrified.

"You look beautiful."

"I look naked."

"Naked and beautiful. For me. You promised. Did you remember a mask?"

"No, but I remembered your present."

I pull the banner from my bag and offer it to her. She tears away the paper and the canvas unspools across her floor. When she sees the painting she gasps and covers her mouth with her hands.

"Oh my god," she says, "oh my god. This is me. You painted me."

"Someday I'll be able to afford a real present."

"You idiot." Her eyes are bright with tears. "How could I want anything other than this? It's the best thing anyone's ever given me."

"Do you remember when your dad's manager got you a pony?"

"Oh, god. That poor fucking thing. It's in a pasture somewhere. Who gets a six-year-old a pony?"

"You did say you wanted one."

"Everyone wants a pony when they're six. That's what's wrong with me, you know? I'm the girl who *got* the pony. Now go downstairs," she adds. "You're not supposed to see the dress before the wedding."

"Nobody's getting married, Aurora."

"God, you are so *literal.*"

I go and find one of the caterers while Aurora gets dressed, and get him to help me hang the banner. I'd thought to put grommets at the corners, and it only takes us a few minutes to secure it in place so that it hangs, waving gently, over the back porch. The sky is purpling. I lean against a pillar, careful not to dirty Aurora's dress, and watch the caterers light tiki torches and mill about, pretending to look busy until the guests arrive. I want to tell them that no one here cares, that they can sit on the grass and drink cocktails if they want. But maybe that's weird. I feel soft hands on my shoulders, and I turn around.

Aurora is wearing a loose, transparent dress made of something cream and gauzy, sewn all over with hundreds of sequins that catch the light and shatter it into a halo around her. Her feet are bare, and her white hair hangs in a sleek curtain down her back. She's outlined her eyes so that they look even bigger, put on a mask of white feathers. She looks inhuman, like some half-bird, half-girl creature who's crossed over to linger, dazzling, in the mortal world. Jack is with her, and I wonder when he got here. Dark clothes to her bright, black hair to her white. They are so glorious I can barely look at them. *Oh, envy,* I think, *you belly full of serpents.* "You look beautiful," I say. I don't know which of them I mean.

I am already drunk when Minos comes. Here in Aurora's house, I think, surely we are safe. I can't erase the image of Jack and Aurora together, Jack's hand at Aurora's waist. Jack leaving. Aurora knew. Who told her? Jack, or Minos? Who told her first? What are they keeping from me? I fill my cup until the edges of the world are fuzzy. Not Minos's eldritch drink; Aurora's perfectly normal vodka. Instead of erasing the world it makes everything worse. I lean on a wall, alone and maudlin in my magical dress. I know who wore it better. Putting pointe shoes on a hippopotamus won't make a fucking ballerina. Jack's avoiding me, and I think if I think about it too much I will crawl under a couch and cry myself into oblivion, so instead I refill my glass. Dance with some boy, masked and courteous, bowing over my hand like we are in a period piece. There are more and more people, people pouring in the front door, clustered around the garden. Some of them I haven't seen in years: old friends of Maia's, of Aurora's dad, their long hair grizzled and their eyes sad behind their masks. None of them recognize me, and I don't bother to say hello.

One minute the party is ordinary, noisy and exuberant, and the next Minos is there. I can feel it before I see him; it's like someone has raised the stage curtains, and now the audience is waiting. The air goes hot and expectant. There are people in masks and people whose masks are not masks, and I am trying again, as always, to tell myself that I am drunk, that I am crazy, but I'm not sure, anymore, that that's true. I lost sight of Aurora and Jack a while ago. Everywhere I go, Minos is there already, watching me, silent, until I want to scream. I run upstairs and into Aurora's room, thinking I will lock myself in, climb into her bed and pull the covers over my head, something, anything.

But he's there, too. Standing by the window, looking out. Aurora's sitting cross-legged in her bed, the feathered mask next to her, and I don't see at first what she is doing. A strip of silk is tied tight around her arm, a syringe in her other hand. *"Aurora."* She looks up, her eyes empty.

"Snakebite," she says dreamily. If I knew how, I would kill him.

"Get out of here," I say, and when he does not move, I say it again. He turns to look at me. His face is somewhere between curious and amused. He lifts one elegant shoulder in a shrug. "Aurora." I shake her. "You know better. Aurora. You idiot."

"Come with me. You promised me we'd be happy." She takes my hand, rests her forehead on my chest. Oh, Aurora. Aurora calling me in the middle of the night, begging me to come get her. Aurora passed out in the garden in her underwear. Aurora with her hands wrapped in my bloody shirt. Aurora at the party, glittering on the precipice. My whole life has been saving Aurora from herself, and there is nowhere she can go where I will not follow. Nothing I will not do to keep her safe. Even this.

"You know you want to," she says. And that's the trick of it, Aurora with her straight shot to my secret heart. For all my protests, all my designated driving, all the nights I've kept on the straight and narrow while she ranged far, I've always wondered what it was like. What was so sweet about that oblivion that it could call our own flesh and blood away from us, send Cass running away from this house and putting Maia on the permanent twilight express. *Goddamn you, Minos, how did you know,* I think, *how did you know?* How badly I want to save her and how badly I want to be her, beautiful and doomed in a pretty dress. How badly I want someone else to do the saving for once. How the fastest way to unravel us was to lay bare our own wants and let them undo us. "Like sisters," Aurora says.

There wouldn't be so many songs about it if it wasn't at least a little bit sweet. "Like always," I say, and kiss her. Minos moves toward me, takes the hand she isn't holding. His touch is as gentle as a lover's. Unbending my arm, bony fingers at the crook of my elbow. The needle the faintest pinch. I close my eyes and wait for what comes next.

I can feel the drug right away, sleek and languid in my veins. Minos's face is as inscrutable as ever, but there is something in those dead eyes that I think is pity. Or maybe it's just contempt. Aurora's room is blurring into darkness, her poster-covered walls fading to black. "Aurora," I whisper, but there's no answer. I have fallen out of the world I know and into something else. There's no sound but the distant murmur of water. I can feel dirt under my bare feet. A chill moves through me. The trees around me are bone-white and bare. I know this place.

In the distance I hear a hectic cacophony, as if a hundred throats are open wide, loosing terrible cries to the unseen sky. The call of horns and the tramp of feet. The noise is growing closer. There's only one path, and I'm standing on it. I look around, frantic, look for somewhere to hide, but there's only the bare trees, the thorns, the blood-colored sap. An unearthly howl rises above the clamor, full of pain and menace, and is joined by another, and another, and then they are upon me.

They are like some nightmare version of a festival parade: a procession of bone-thin riders on horses so dark I can only see them as empty cutouts of night against the white trees. The riders are maggot-white, the white of fungus and old bone. They're still in their party masks: fur and feathers, velvet and lace, rotting silk and dirty satin. Their long ragged hair is braided with tattered dark ribbons that flutter madly although there is no wind. They radiate a greenish light that does nothing to push away the impermeable night. They stream past me, slow and stately. I cower against a white trunk, taking care not to catch myself on the huge thorns, but the riders take no notice of me. *I am in Aurora's room. I am on Aurora's bed.* But I can feel the cold smooth trunk under my hands, can smell the faint tang of rust and rot that comes from the riders. My bare feet are cold and goosebumps are rising on my skin. I pinch myself and nothing happens. Pinch harder. Bite down on my lip until my mouth floods with the bitter taste of blood, and still the riders keep coming. That trio of howls again, so close now they make me jump, and in that jerky unguarded movement my shoulder hits one of the thorny vines and I cry out as the spikes pierce my skin. Hissing in pain, I look up and see Minos.

He's astride the biggest horse I've ever seen. He is wearing a dark robe of some kind of fur and a crown of twisted metal set with cracked and dirty red stones. Aurora is behind him, arms tight around him, head resting on his back, eyes closed, her hair a beacon in all that dark. At the horse's feet trots a huge black dog with three heads. One of the heads turns toward me, and the dog stops, its three muzzles thrust into the air and sniffing, like some horrible parody of a house pet searching out treats. Three sets of teeth, ridged fangs each as long as my thumb; three red tongues dripping with slaver; three growls rising in three hot throats. Minos halts the massive horse. The riders split around him as seamlessly as water, flow back together once they've passed him and stream away down the path. I see Jack, sitting tall on a horse of his own, surrounded by ghouls. His head is held high and his back rigid. His guitar is slung across his chest. His face is a mask, his mouth a straight line. "Jack!" I shriek. "Jack!" But he doesn't turn, doesn't look toward me. The horse moves relentlessly away until he's lost in a sea of black.

The dog howls, the same trio of howls I heard in the distance. Minos holds out a bony hand and the dog stops, looks up at him with a tripled gaze that is equal parts adoration and fear. It wags its whip-thin tail and moves away from me. Minos is as still as stone, watching me, the endless riders moving around him, the dog sitting now, expectant, waiting for a command. "You can't have her," I say. "You can't have either of them." Aurora opens her eyes, sees me, her face aglow.

"You came," she says. "I knew you'd come. We're going to see my dad now." The pain in my shoulder is spreading. I take a shaky step toward Minos, but my body is burning up. He bares his teeth as if he's going to take a bite out of me, and I realize he is smiling. Aurora's gaze goes unfocused, her mouth slack. "Oh," she whispers. "It's so beautiful down here." Her lids flutter closed.

"You fucker," I snarl. "Give her back." The world around me is dimming, a red haze moving across my vision. I take another step forward and fall to my knees. Minos puts his heels to the horse and beckons to the dog. I stagger to my feet. The last of the riders thunder past me. I can hear the echo of hooves far ahead. There's no way out but forward. Each step is more painful than the last.

When I get to the river I sink to my knees again, touch my forehead to the colorless earth in despair. There is no sign of them. I hear the dog's howl, muffled as though it comes now from somewhere deep in the earth. Faint but unmistakable, the first chords as Jack begins to play. *Go home, child,* someone says, and darkness comes down around me like a curtain.

I open my eyes to green. The smell of wet earth fills my nose. I'm freezing and my body is one giant ache. Somewhere above me a bird scolds me with a vigorous, descending trill. I push myself up on my elbows, wincing at the stab of pain in my shoulder. I'm in the trampled, empty wreckage of Aurora's yard, sopping wet, tangled in the shredded ruins of her dress and covered in fresh-cut grass. The sky is the white-gold of dawn. I climb shakily to my feet and check for damage. Ten fingers, ten toes, bum shoulder, wobbly legs. Otherwise in full working order.

The inside of the house is a disaster. Streamers hang crazily from the huge chandelier, and the front hall is caked with mud and feathers, bits of fur, the broken pieces of a jeweled necklace with its gems cracked and smeared with filth. Paintings hang at odd angles, the glass in their frames splintered into jagged starbursts. My heart catches when I see the banner I painted for Aurora, torn down and trampled. I pick it up out of the dirt, brush off the worst of the grime, but it's ruined. I leave it on the back porch and go inside again. "Maia?" I call, climbing the sweeping staircase to the second floor, but there's no answer.

I peek in Aurora's room, hoping against hope that she's here, lounging in her bed, chugging Dr Pepper and eating Slim Jims and watching eighties movies. Painting her toenails and rolling her eyes at me, demanding to know where I've been. Her room's empty, the bed unmade and strewn with eyeliner pencils and lipsticks. The syringe winks at me from the covers where we must have left it. I rub the crook of my elbow and shiver. There's not even a mark there.

I open Aurora's drawers as if she's hiding inside them. Just a welter of crocheted bikinis and silk slips, fishnets, a rhinestone necklace. A pair of ancient ballet shoes left over from our brief stint as ballerinas when we were still in the single digits. A paper covered in Cass's handwriting: Aurora's horoscope, undated. *Mars is less happy in Taurus.* Great, Cass, very helpful. Exactly what Aurora needs. I walk down the hall to Maia's room.

I think, for a second, that this time Maia really is dead. She's out cold on her bed, her eyes closed, her skin ashen. A few stragglers from the party are passed out in various states of disarray. There's a long-haired dude next to her, one arm hanging off the bed, as comatose as she is. "Shit," I whisper, but then I see the faint rise and fall of her bony chest. "Maia," I say, but she's zombied. I say it again, louder. I don't want to touch her, but I swallow hard and shake her. Her eyelids flutter.

"Aurora?" she murmurs.

"No such luck. Maia, do you need a doctor?" At last she opens her eyes and gives me an unfocused stare.

"You're not Aurora."

"We covered that. We're moving past 101 now. Are you okay, Maia? Do you need to go to the hospital?" She looks bad but not dying. She looks the same way she's looked for most of the last decade, minus a bit of zest. I sit on the bed, take her hand. "Maia? How you doing, lady? When did you eat last? How much smack did you do last night?"

"Where's Aurora?"

"She either went to Los Angeles or she went to hell."

"What?" But Maia's barely conscious. She's more pitiable than anything. Her complete failure to rise to the occasion comes as no surprise. I think of all the times she told us how she was going to get sober, how this time it would be for real. This time she was going to go to a spa in the hills of California, drink lemon juice and hot water for ten straight days, return pure and clear. This time she was going to backpack into the desert, eat peyote and let the spirits take the drugs out of her. This time she was going to stay with some friends on a sailboat, head north to the islands along the coast, learn how to fish. This time she was going to buy a cabin on the beach in Mexico, spend the winters there until the sun bleached all the junk out of her veins. This time, this time, this time. But it always turned into next time, or the time after. Always something came up, something happened. Some old friend came to visit. Some hard day. Some reminder. "This is the day I met your father," she'd tell Aurora, and then she'd disappear into her room and we wouldn't see her for days. This day was the day Aurora's father died. This day was the day Aurora's father's bassist told Maia he never wanted to see her again, that she'd been the one who ruined everything. That if it hadn't been for her the band would still be together and no one would be dead. Every day contained some moment that made this time the time that didn't count. Next time, next time she'd get clean for real. *Oh, Maia.* I smooth her greasy hair away from her forehead. Music is playing, so faint it's only now registering. It's the remastered album the record label put out, a decade after Aurora's dad died. All of us hate this album. "Fucking producers," Aurora said, the first time we listened to it. I never heard her play it again.

"I guess Aurora went away for a while," I say to Maia now, my voice catching. "I wanted to make sure you were okay. Do you think you should take a shower or something?"

"Did you have fun at the party?" Her head lolls back on her neck.

"Not really." The man in her bed mutters, rolls over. Score another point for the living.

"I saw him," she says. "I saw him here. Why was he here?"

"Who did you see, Maia?"

"The skeleton man." My whole body goes cold.

"Do you mean Minos? How do you know Minos?"

"That asshole. He was always around." She lifts her head with an effort. "Always around," she repeats, her voice slurry. "Always making promises. Everyone was going to be so goddamn rich. Everything we ever wanted. I could have had him forever. He used to write me songs; did Cass ever tell you that? Before that stupid album. We were so fucking happy and we couldn't even see it. Look at me now. Listen to this shit." She points in the general direction of the stereo. "Don't let Aurora—" She falters. "Don't let him take her away. He has the best drugs. I can never say no when he's here. He told me—last night he told me . . ." She trails off.

"Who else did he take away? Maia? Who else?"

"Who do you think?" She struggles to sit up and I reach forward to help her, but she bats my hands away. "Fucking Cass," she mutters. "Cass let him in. Cass tried to take my baby, too. You tell Cass I said she can go to hell."

"Cass wasn't here last night," I say.

"Not last night. A long time ago."

"Cass let Aurora's dad in?"

"You aren't listening to me."

"Maia. I don't understand what you're telling me. Where did Aurora go? Do you know? Did she go to California?"

"It's too late," Maia says, and starts to cry. "If she went

with him, it's too late. Now I have to go looking for her, too."

"Tell me how to find her. Tell me where they went. Tell me what Cass did." But she's leaning back into the pillows, coughing, her eyes closing.

"I have to sleep. I can see him sometimes when I sleep."

"Maia. *Maia*." Her face is still. I wait for her to say something else, but she is gone again, to wherever it is that she goes. I shut the door behind me and go to find some clothes. I am not looking forward to the bike ride home.

My apartment is empty, the breakfast dishes washed and drying in the drainer. I have no idea what to do with myself, stand stupidly in the middle of my room staring out the window. I don't have to work today. If it were any other day, a normal day, I'd be at the beach with Aurora. Post-morteming her party, talking shit about the guests. Who wore what and who paired off, locking themselves in her bathroom for way too long. Aurora nursing her hangover with a bag of Doritos and a raw egg in tomato juice, me making horrified faces while she insists it's the healthiest cure imaginable. Later, I'd call Jack, and we'd have a picnic in the park or stay up all night in his little house, kissing with the windows open to let the night in. But none of that, now.

I can't remember the last time I went running. I unbutton the shirt I stole from Aurora's closet, wincing at the sharp twinge in my shoulder. I check out my back in my mirror and there it is: an ugly constellation of red punctures, the flesh around them puffy and discolored. I wonder what happens if they get infected, if there's some kind of first aid manual for the cuts you get in hell. I put on my sports bra and a T-shirt, doing my best not to touch the wounds.

Outside, I lace up my sneakers and start to run. Head down, legs moving, harder and faster than I've ever run before. Running away from last night, the pain in my shoulder, the memory of that river of ghouls carrying Jack and Aurora away from me. I don't pay attention to where I'm going, don't look up even when I crash into a couple pushing a toddler in a stroller. Their startled squawks follow me as I keep going. I run until I think my knees will split apart, until my mouth is open and working and the air is hot on my dried-out tongue. I run until I trip over a rough patch of sidewalk and go flying, the breath coming out of me in a sharp whoosh as I hit the ground full-on. I lie there for a minute, stunned, so winded I wonder if I'm going to throw up, and then I roll over on my side. "Jesus," someone says. "Are you okay?" A middle-aged man in a suit is standing over me, his expression anxious. "Do you need me to call someone?" Laboriously, I get to my feet.

"I'm fine," I whisper, when I can catch my breath enough to get the words out. "Thanks."

"You—I think you—I think you might need to go to the hospital." He points. I look down. The skin on my knees and elbows is gone.

"Seriously," I wheeze. "This happens all the time. Thanks."

"I can—"

"I'm fucking *fine*." He backs away.

"I was only trying to help," he says, curt now.

"I don't need your fucking help! I need my fucking friends!" I don't care how I look, and I don't care what's coming out of my mouth. Nothing has ever felt as good as screaming at this total stranger. "I need my best friend! I need my best friend's mom to quit doing drugs! I need parents and I need my boyfriend back and I need Aurora's dad to not be a dead fuckup rock star and I need that creepy asshole to leave me and the people I love alone and I need—" Gasping, I run out of steam. The businessman is gaping at me. "Shit," I mutter. "Sorry. Bad day." I turn around and limp away. My mouth is so dry it's burning. I would kill someone for a glass of water. A businessman. I would kill a businessman for a glass of water. Ha ha.

I walk for a long time without thinking. When I look around I'm standing in front of the big old cathedral at the edge of downtown. Why not? My feet whisper across the red carpet. I'm so thirsty I dip one hand into the marble basin of holy water, make a cup out of my palm, and bring the droplets to my mouth. A lady clutching a rosary next to me hisses in disapproval. The water doesn't taste like anything. Overhead the cathedral's arching ribs meet in a dizzying peak, and the light fractures through the stained-glass windows. People file past me, genuflecting at their pews and sliding into their seats, kneeling in prayer.

I stand in the nave, watching as the priest in his rich white robe edged in gold raises his hands over the congregation, and people begin to sing in Latin. The dead language swirls around me and the sun blazes behind, casting my shadow in a long strip across the red carpet. A few people turn around to look at me, and then keep staring. Someone who looks official—what do you call people who work at a church? They can't all be the ones who don't have sex, some of them must be secretaries or something—turns to the man next to him and mimes making a phone call. That's for sure my cue to split. I stumble back out into the innocuous afternoon, and then there is nothing left to do but go home.

Cass is sitting at the kitchen table with a mug of tea, the light streaming in around her in buttery slabs. When she sees me she starts.

"What happened to you? You're a holy mess." She grabs a clean dishtowel, runs it under the tap, sits me down at the kitchen table. I wince as the skin stretches over my abraded knees. She dabs at me with the towel. I push her away.

"Sweetheart, you look awful. Let me clean you up, okay?"

"They went without me." She sets the towel aside and puts her arms around me.

"Who went without you?"

"Jack and Aurora."

"Where did they go?"

"Wherever he took them." I start to cry. She doesn't ask me who I mean. She holds me while I sob into her shirt, rocking me gently like she used to do when I was small enough to fit on her lap. She doesn't try to hush me, or tell me everything will be okay. She lets me cry until I have no tears left, and then she gets up and pours me a cup of tea and pushes the mug toward me. I stare at my reflection in the sweet-smelling liquid.

"What do I do now? How do I find them?"

"I don't know, baby. I don't know."

All the days after that pass in an indistinct blur. I catch Cass filling bowls with crystals and salt water and leaving them on the windowsills. She unearths the dog-eared paperback with her spell recipes and mutters incantations over colored candles, pours drops of oil in the corners of every room, burns so many herbs she sets off the smoke alarm. I lay out my tarot cards over and over, but I don't even know what question to ask. I find one of Aurora's white hairs across my pillow, and a guitar pick in a bowl of apples. After that, nothing. I listen to Nick Cave over and over because it feels true. *I let love in. I let love in.* So much there that's not love, so much there that's anger. Love and hate are twins. I listen to songs about following your wife into the dark beneath the earth, the music that leads you there. *Oh mama.* I was such a fool. Such a fool to think I could have either one of them, to think that Jack loved me, to think that there was anything real but the two of them together and me on the outside, looking in.

I sleep for what feels like days. Years. The entire rest of my life. I sleep so much that when I'm awake I don't feel right and the edges of my vision go furry. I dream about her, always, all the time. Aurora in the ocean, her white hair floating behind her. Aurora in a house like a palace, white walls, white-hot sky. Aurora, huge dark eyes looking back at me out of a pool in the earth ringed with flowers. Aurora with Minos's long bony fingers around her throat. One night I can see her again with the syringe, the strip of silk. She's in a bathtub the size of a fish pond. Marble-floored bathroom, candles everywhere. Floor-to-ceiling windows and beyond them black sea, black sky. I can see the steam rising off the bathwater, smell lavender and salt breeze and the rich vanilla of Aurora's skin. She's skinnier than ever, barely any flesh on her long bones, the line of her cheek knife-sharp. Her white hair like a beacon in the dark. Her lips part and her eyes roll back in her head. She's sliding underwater, down, down, down. *No!* I cry, and reach for her, but she's too far away for me to touch. *You left me,* she whispers. *You let me go.* And then she's gone and I jerk awake, dripping with sweat, in my own dirty sheets, my own bed, my own shabby apartment. Our kingdom glimmers on the far wall, the country that we made together. "Aurora," I say aloud into the dark, but there's no one there to hear. "Aurora. I'm sorry. Come back."

Cass tiptoes around me, takes to leaving my meals outside the door of my room. I don't want to eat, but the smell lures me out like a bear to bait. Betrayed again by my animal body and its stupid animal wants: food, friendship, sex, love. Cass and I don't talk. I'm a chalkboard that's been erased over and over again until there's nothing left but a haze of white dust. Before this I never understood how long an hour could take, how many ticks of the second hand are in a minute, how endless the space between seconds can be.

I can never put together a whole picture of Jack in my head. Shoulders, hips, the line of his belly, the muscles of his back. The soft place behind his knee. Long tendons in his forearms, long fingers, long narrow toes. Sunlight throwing bone into relief: the sharp place at the inside of his elbow, the bird-fine bones of his wrist, the muscles of his thigh moving under his skin like water. The tangle of his hair. I draw pieces of him and tape them together, take them apart again. I draw a single line and already it's wrong. I draw the angle of his cheek. I draw his palms the way I remember them, but on paper they are nothing I recognize. My desk is piled with crumpled sheets of newsprint, my fingers covered in charcoal dust. Jack cutting fruit in his kitchen, frozen with his knife parting the apple's green skin. Jack playing me Leonard Cohen songs on his porch, the birds in his garden creeping forward to listen better. Jack in my room, laughing, shirt unbuttoned. Jack watching me draw. Jack's voice in my ear, low and rough. I don't know if it's worse to have a thing like that and then have it taken away from you or to never have a thing like that at all.

My brain's not shy about coming up with other images that, for all I know, are just as real: Jack and Aurora hand in hand on the California beach, Jack and Aurora in a convertible with the top down, drinking margaritas by the ocean and watching the sun set. Did they go away for Minos, or did they go away for each other? Did they go to get away from me? Does Jack know by now that Aurora loves anchovies and olives on her pizza but would die before touching pineapple, that she drinks her coffee with so much sugar it's a wonder she has any teeth left? Does he know that *The Lost Boys* reminds her of her dad for no rational reason? Does he know she learned French so she could read Rimbaud in the original? Has she told him we used to take turns reading *The Dark Is Rising* aloud to each other every Christmas? Does he have his motorcycle wherever he is now and are they together, her arms around his waist, her hair whipping back from her helmet, are they driving down Highway 1 to Mexico like Jack and I said we were going to do, are they sleeping on the beach and watching the sun rise over the Pacific and learning all the constellations? Is he cutting her slices of peach with his knife, feeding them to her one by one? Does he touch her the same way he touched me? Are they lost, or lonely, and do they think of me, and if he has kissed her does he wish it is me he is kissing, or has her perfect face already wiped mine from his memory? Does he touch her the way he touched me? Every night I go over to my window and look out, at the spot in the shadows where I thought I'd seen Minos before, but the street is empty and dark and even the shadows have no weight. I'm not who he was waiting for.

Does he touch her the way he touched me.

At work, Raoul knocks gently on my skull. Anyone home? No. He covers for me while I sit on a crate, staring out over purple mounds of plums. He mothers me back to his apartment, feeds me soup, puts Oscar Wilde on my head to make me laugh. It's the only thing that works. We smoke pot and watch television and when he brings me more and more snacks I realize he's getting me stoned so I'll eat. I tell him I don't deserve him, and he hushes me.

"Everyone needs to be loved through their first broken heart," he says, and I love him so much I can hardly stand to look at him. I tell him what Jack said to me before he left.

"I bet they're there together. I bet they wanted to be together this whole time. I bet she—"

"Why would you say a thing like that?" Raoul interrupts.

"Because everyone falls in love with her. She can't even help it. It's not her fault. She wanted him and she got him and now they're probably in Los Angeles laughing at me."

"Did you ever think that maybe Aurora loves Jack because he's the only person in her life who doesn't want anything from her?"

"I don't want anything from her," I say, stung.

"Are you sure?"

"I tried to protect her."

"Did you? Or did you just want an excuse to follow where she was already going?"

"Raoul. I love her."

"I know you do, but love can make us do ugly things, too. Sometimes I think you don't really see her; you see the same thing everyone else sees when they look at her. Something ornamental. Underneath, though, she's just as real and hurt as you are."

"But Jack and Aurora have this kind of magic. I'll never have whatever it is that makes them what they are." Raoul opens his mouth to protest, but I cut him off. "It's fine. I don't mind. I mean, I do mind. But it is what it is. I wish sometimes it came that easily for me, too. It's hard not to be jealous."

"I don't think it's easy," he says. "Not for Jack, and certainly not for Aurora."

"How can it not be easy for Aurora? Look at her."

"That's what I mean," he says. "Look at her. Look at both of them. Do you ever think about what a curse it might be, to look like that? To know that no matter what you were made of, no matter what you did with your life, no one would ever see past your face? Your skin?"

"What does that have to do with Jack leaving me for Aurora?"

"Now you're not listening to me, either." For the first time, he's angry. I feel a hot surge of hurt and open my mouth to say something, close it again. "Just think about it," he says. "For me."

"Do you feel like that?"

"All the time," he says simply. "I mean, I write poetry, so there's not much chance I'll have to make a choice like Jack did, but if it ever happens I know what it will be like. Do I see myself as a poet or as a brown poet or as a queer poet, as if all of those things are separate boxes I check depending on what day of the week it is. If I write about my family, people will ask me why I don't write poetry that's relatable, and if I don't write about my family, they'll ask me how I can stand to betray my roots. If I write about nature people will tell me how moving it is that my people are so connected to the earth. If I write about the city people will tell me how brave I am for talking about the realities of the urban experience. And none of those people will actually read the words I write. Everyone lives with it differently. Some people push it down so far inside they think it can't hurt them, and it festers there. Some people talk about it. Some people don't. Jack told you he was making the best decision he knew how to make in the circumstances he has to deal with. He has something people want, and it's up to him to decide how he gives it to them. How he lets them take it."

"But it was selfish."

"All the best artists are selfish. You can't be good unless you care about the work more than you care about anything else."

"But what about *me*?" As soon as I say it I want to take it back. This is the most Raoul has ever said to me about anything serious, this is the biggest thing he has ever trusted me with, and all I can do is come out of it sounding like a spoiled child. But with that hanging in the air between us,

I see what Raoul has been trying to tell me. What Jack was trying to tell me. "Oh," I say. "It's not about me at all."

"No."

I cover my eyes with my hands. I always thought Aurora could metabolize love the way she can metabolize Dr Pepper and vodka and bad speed, that it passed through her without marking her and left only more emptiness in its wake. I have known her as long as I have known myself; there is no story of me without her written in every chapter. But now for the first time I wonder if the flaw isn't hers, but mine. If all along it was me taking without thinking, not her. If what Aurora has given me isn't infinitely more priceless than what I've given her, and if now I'm letting her slide into darkness without a fight because it's easier than bringing my own faults into the light.

"Why are you always right," I mumble into my palms.

"I do a lot of thinking."

"It hurts," I say. "It hurts a lot."

"I know it does. And it doesn't mean Jack doesn't love you. It just means there are bigger things than you. Jack's allowed to love music more than he loves you. I know it's hard to hear, but that doesn't make it any less true. That's what he said, isn't it?"

"Pretty much."

"Then there's not much you can do about it except choose how you're going to deal with it. You can hate him for it, or you can figure out how to let him go."

"I don't want to let him go. I want him back. I want both of them back."

"Indeed," he says. "There's the rub."

SEPTEMBER

After everything that's happened, it's hard to believe in high school, but that doesn't mean I don't have to go. It's only September, but the summer's ended as swiftly as a doused fire. The first morning of school is so cold the sidewalk outside my building is rimed with frost. I put on a ratty black hoodie over my rattiest shirt and rattiest pair of black jeans, run my fingers through my ratty hair, lace up my ratty combat boots. Ratty fingerless gloves and a ratty wool beanie and a ratty down vest. Jack used to joke he'd pay me to wear a color other than black. I tug the hood of my sweatshirt up over the beanie. Maybe if I turtle down far enough into it I'll disappear altogether.

I bike to school with my headphones in my ears, even though Cass always tells me I'll get killed that way, listening to an old Earth album cranked up as loud as a headache. Coming down the last hill, I hit a patch of ice and the back wheel skids out from under me before I know what's happening. I land flat on my back, somehow manage not to crack my skull on the ground. I'm starting a trend: the full-on wipeout, by foot or by wheel. Awesome. I lie in the street for a moment, stunned. Maybe another hapless suit will wander past and I can scream my head off at him, too.

I pick myself up, check for damage. There's a hole in my sleeve and my neck hurts. No one saw me, for which I'm grateful. Bike's fine, wheels still true, but I walk it the rest of the way to school anyway, limping as the pain sets in. I'll have hefty war wounds and no one to show them off to.

High school has gotten no less prisonlike over the summer. I'm a senior now, officially at the top of the totem pole, building memories and planning for my future. No one bothered to clean the hallways over summer break. Dark smears of spilled soda and other, more mysterious fluids have dried to a gummy residue that absorbs the lurid fluorescent light and gives the linoleum floors a three-dimensional effect. I slouch from class to class, sit in the back, keep my head down and speak only when spoken to. Which is, thanks to the halo of menace I radiate, pretty much never. Between classes I jam my headphones back into my ears and glare. People look at me, look away quickly, and then glance back. They want to know why Aurora's ray of sunshine isn't around to offset my personal cloud of doom. Want to know why we aren't joined at the hip, cutting class to smoke in the parking lot or get stoned with the metalheads behind the gym. Aurora making eyes at everyone, Aurora in her ridiculous clothes, Aurora dancing by herself on the football field, not caring who sees her, not caring that the music is in her head.

At lunch, some girl from my homeroom sidles up to me with a puppy face. "What." I take off my headphones.

"I was just wondering, you know, where Aurora was."

"Not here."

"Is she having a back-to-school party?"

"Do you see anything to celebrate?"

She stares at me, and I put my headphones back on. That's the last time anyone tries to talk to me for a week.

I pull my Bartleby routine like cheer has gone out of style. Even in art class I'm sullen. The teacher is new this year, some fresh-out-of-college stoner who can't quite hide his hanker for the choicer meats of the senior class. I refuse to participate in his earnest still lifes, leaving my sketchbook ostentatiously blank and staring out the window, or drawing weird landscapes peopled with stag-headed men moving through the shadows when I'm supposed to be drawing a vase and an apple. On Friday, Cass pounces as I slink through the door after work. My hours at the market are patches of post-school heaven. Raoul won't let me mope. He tells me jokes, tugs my hair, makes eyes at the fish-stall boys in front of me. I'm almost in a good mood by the time I get home.

"I got a call from the school." Cass points me to the couch. I collapse in a sulky pile.

"About?"

"What do you think?" She perches on the edge of an arm-chair we once reupholstered in scraps of tapestry. They're fraying now. Like everything. I chew on my fingers and fidget. She tries to stare me down, but I refuse to meet her eyes.

"Look, baby. I know this is hard, but there's nothing you can do. If they want to come back, they'll come back. If you don't bring up your grades, you won't get into art school."

"We can't afford art school."

"All the more reason not to alienate the person respon-sible for recommending you for scholarships, don't you think?"

"I really miss them."

"I know you do. I miss Aurora, too. But you're not doing anyone any good by turning into a little gothic nightmare. Your art teacher is terrified of you."

"He's an idiot."

"I'm sure he is, but you're not, and there's no reason to burn a bridge that might lead to a happier place. You really want to spend the rest of your life hustling fruit and shack-ing up with your hippie mom?"

"The horror." I let a smile through. Throw her a bone.

"So we'll put our game face on, shall we?" I shrug. Her hand whips forward and seizes my chin. "I said, shall we?"

"Yes," I mutter, and her grip tightens. "Yes!" I yelp. "Jesus." She releases me and I flee for the safety of my room. After that, I draw the vases and the apples and Cass leaves me alone.

It's hard to believe I didn't imagine the entire summer. Every morning I put on gloves and a beanie and two hoodies before I ride to school. The cheerleaders make a show of displaying their tans in short shorts and cropped jackets, but even they give up the fight after one too many days clustered together in the hallway like a gaggle of plucked chickens, prickling with goosebumps.

Fall is usually my favorite season. I love the sharp clear days, the smell of fallen leaves, even the lurking menace of winter with its endless rains around the corner. I love spending long afternoons with Aurora, drinking coffee until our fingers twitch and watching the sky grow dark a little earlier each day, borrowing her cashmere sweaters and biker jackets, stomping around in my tallest boots. I love that feeling of cocooning inward. Aurora hates any weather in which she cannot be constantly naked, but she's always gone along with my enthusiasm, trying to knit scarves or make soup or take up weaving or some other project she's constitutionally unsuited for. She never fails to leave off in the middle, with predictably disastrous results. She nearly set her house on fire the night she tried to make me minestrone. It was supposed to be a surprise, and then she forgot about it, and the soup burned down to a puck of coal while we watched *Fast Times at Ridgemont High* in her bed, and it wasn't until we smelled smoke that she yelled, "Shit! Shit!" and catapulted downstairs to a blackened, toxic mess. She threw it, pot and all, in the yard, where it stayed for weeks.

But now she's gone, and so is Jack, and with them my dreams of piling up together in Jack's house, the three of us watching rain fall against the windows and drinking tea and reading books out loud to one another. Later, Jack and I falling asleep under a pile of blankets, safe from the storm thundering overhead, skin to skin. Him writing me songs and me painting him pictures. This hazy fantasy does not include such trivial details as school, or work, or the fact that I still live with my mother. Cass has her quirks, but worrying about sex and nights away from home isn't one of them. I could probably have worked around her as long as I came home for dinner sometimes. But none of that is going to happen now. I scuff through the fallen leaves on my own.

I go to shows without Aurora, feeling like half of me is missing. I hand over my fake ID and watch as the guys working the door look around me, waiting for her. I slam-dance at the front of the pit, throwing myself up against sweaty shirtless boys who punch me back when I punch them. Afterward I let them shove me up against the wall in the alley or the bathroom and kiss me, push their hands up under my clothes. When I kiss them back I bite down until I draw blood. Less like sex and more like a fistfight, dirty and mean. It feels good. In those moments I forget about Jack and Aurora at last, forget about everything except my body's need for harder, faster, louder, bigger, bigger, more. I wear scarves to school, never let Cass see my bruise-colored skin, go to all my classes and keep my eyes open and then do it all over again. When the music stops the hole inside me is so huge I think I might die from it.

Without Aurora to watch over, I'm free to get as drunk as I want, to fuck up and fuck up again. Free to say yes to anything, to all the bad ideas. Free to slam so hard in the pit my teeth hurt, to let anyone in. One night I meet a boy I've never seen before. Brown doe eyes in a hard face. I can't tell which is the true part, whether the gentleness in his eyes is real or a mask. He asks me my name. "Aurora," I say.

"That's pretty." He buys me a drink, and then another one. Is this what it feels like to be beautiful? Is this what it feels like to know everyone is watching you, everyone wants what's under your skin? I can't ask her because she's not here. But if she were here, no one would look at me first. Later, I let the boy kiss me in the back of his van, yank my jeans down, shove his way inside. He licks my ear and it's supposed to be sexy. His breath smells like beer and unbrushed teeth. I close my eyes. If I concentrate hard enough I can be back at the park, that very first night. The night I met Jack and everything started to fall apart. "Aurora," he grunts in my ear. "Aurora, Aurora." I think for a minute he is saying her name because she is here, in the front seat, smoking, rolling her eyes. *Come on, babycakes, let's go.* But when I open my eyes the night is real and his van smells like cigarettes and old takeout and my legs are cold despite the press of his body, and I am all the way alone.

"Get off me."

"What?"

"Get the fuck *off* me." I shove him over, wriggle out from under him, zip up my jeans. Try not to think about the blanket underneath me or where it's been.

"That's not what you were saying a minute ago." In that moment I have never hated another human being so much in my life. If I stay here I'll put out his eyes with my thumbs.

"I have to go."

"Will I see you again?"

"You better hope not." I open the door of his van and stumble out into the night.

There is no one to look out for me except Raoul. If I call him, if I need him, he'll come for me, but I like feeling as though I am falling into darkness so wide no one will be able to see when I hit the bottom. I'll be out of sight before they even know where to look. Going, going, gone.

I ride past Jack's house on my way home from work a few nights later. I stop my bike in the street outside, half-hoping to see lights inside, maybe even him sitting on the front porch playing guitar in the cold. But the jungle of vines in his front yard has withered into desiccated husks that snag at my clothes as I push my bike down the walkway. His flowers are reduced to rank brown piles that give off a sour smell of rot. His spare key is still in its spot under a loose brick. I hold it for a moment, thinking, and then I let myself in.

The bed is unmade and there are dirty dishes in the sink, dregs in a coffee cup furred over with mold. Clothes on the floor, a pair of his boots leaning against each other in the corner. The emptiness in the room is so thick I can taste it. The house is cold. A draft stirs against my cheek. The window is open. I'm already inside; might as well keep going. I cross the room and shut the window against the night air. Run my finger across the card table. My fingertip comes back grey with dust. One corner of the Rousseau poster has come loose from the wall and dangles forlornly. If there is a magic trick that will bring Jack back to me, its instructions are not here.

I pick up a shirt off the floor. Worn flannel with a hole in one elbow. I remember him in it. It's the shirt he was wearing the night I read his cards. I slip my arms into the sleeves, wrap it around me. The cuffs dangle past my knuckles. If this were the kind of story I want to be in, he'd have left something for me. A note under the pillow, a charm under a loose floorboard. A box of talismans, a salve for sore losers. If this were the kind of story I want to be in, I'd have a trail of breadcrumbs to follow, a message written in invisible ink that I only needed to shine a light on to make the words real. Better yet, the quest would end here and he'd be waiting for me, sitting on his bed, wondering where I'd been. He'd tell me he was sorry, that what mattered most was not the music, not the outside world, not what he had come here to seek out, but what he had found in me. That we could spend the rest of our lives here in this room, learning all each other's stories, learning the patterns of our bodies, the rhythms of our breath. If this were the kind of story I want to be in, I'd flip back to the pages where all the words made sense and the ending wasn't written yet.

His bed still smells like him, honey and sweat. I crawl between the covers, put my head on the dirty pillow. His shirt, his bed, his house. His absence is so strong it has a texture. *You asshole,* I think. *You weren't supposed to leave me behind.* But in my head Aurora's face overlaps his, the edges blurring, until I can't tell which one of them is standing in front of me, waiting for me to follow. I am at the edge of the river again, the bone trees all around me. I see the flash of her white hair on the far bank, hear the passing music of a single chord, and then nothing. I am standing, barefoot and bloody, knowing Aurora and Jack are ahead of me somewhere in the dark. They have gone on together and I am lost on this, the opposite side.

I wake up a few hours later with a start, not sure where I am for long moments. I don't remember crying, but my face is tracked with salt. The room has the spare, washed-thin feel of very early morning. Outside, a misty rain is falling. I take Jack's shirt and leave everything else as it is. Dirty dishes, books with cracked spines, unmade bed, silence. I ride home in the damp night, in and out of the pooled light of streetlamps.

I let myself into the apartment as quietly as I can. Cass's door is closed. No bar of light seeps out the bottom, but there's a plate of muffins in the kitchen that still carry a trace of the oven's heat. I eat one standing over the sink, tearing it apart with my fingers into smaller and smaller pieces, soft chunks of apple tangy-sweet in my mouth. If I keep doing nothing I will lose my mind. In my room I take off all my clothes, shivering, and then put Jack's flannel on again. The fabric is soft against my skin, the smell of him somehow stronger. I put my hand between my legs. No matter how hard I try I cannot quite picture his face.

OCTOBER

t's the week before Halloween when I see the poster. I bike a roundabout way to school that morning, wanting to put off the inevitable as long as possible despite the gentle, half-hearted rain that mists down in a chilly cloud. I'm listening to the same Earth album I've been playing for weeks, the sludgy wall of guitar soothing me as I pedal, like a metalhead version of those tapes of whale songs and crashing waves that are supposed to help you fall asleep. I smoke a joint in the morning now, on the days I go to school, and another one at lunch, until I'm so stoned I'm moving around in my own impermeable bubble, my thoughts stilled into silence.

Aurora and I love Halloween best of all the holidays. I always pretend to be lazy and disinclined to find a costume, and she makes a great fuss about it and berates me for my indifference; but of course secretly I love the ritual of her convincing me every year, and she knows it. Aurora's a magnificent scavenger, a holy terror in thrift stores and secondhand shops, with a magpie's eye for glitter and an unerring instinct for hidden treasure buried among the detritus of molting down jackets and dog-eared paperbacks. What I lack in thrifting skills I make up for in the kind of single-minded, tenacious patience that allowed me to sew hundreds of white feathers to a set of leotards the year Aurora decided we should be owls, or stud a pair of denim jackets with so many fake gemstones they were as heavy as armor the year we went as Jem and a singular Hologram. Aurora smokes out my window while I work, drinking coffee and nattering at me and pretending to help. She throws glorious parties every year, legendary parties—ice sculptures of monsters dotting the yard, the whole house done up like a haunted mansion with cobwebs and people leaping at you out of darkened hallways, dressed as mummies or vampires or corpses with their flesh peeling away. This year, without her, it's like the color has gone out of the world, and the growing tribe of jack-o'-lanterns grinning from front porches and windows only serves to remind me of what I've lost.

I'm waiting at an intersection when I see the poster out of the corner of my eye. I swing a leg off my bike and walk it over. The paper is faded and stained, one corner missing, but there's no mistaking Jack's name, or the name of the club, or the date. Halloween. Four days away.

I stand there for a long time, as the light changes and then changes again. A man leans out his car window. "Hey kid, you okay? You got a flat?" I turn, and he sees my face. "You okay?" he says again.

"I'm fine." Forever pestered by earnest middle-aged men longing to help and destined to be spurned. He's driving a minivan; he's probably used to it. The car behind him honks, and he shrugs and drives away. I tear the poster off the telephone pole, fold it into smaller and smaller squares. Stuff it in my pocket. I have three days to decide what I'm going to do about it.

That night, Cass makes us curry. I chop vegetables while she sautés tofu, puts a pot of brown rice on the stove to simmer. "I saw a poster for a show Jack's playing," I say. Casual. No big deal.

"Where?"

"Los Angeles. I'm going to find a way to go. I'm sure Aurora is there."

She raises an eyebrow at me, incredulous. "Oh you are, are you? This event taking place over my dead body?"

"What do you care?" I'm traveling fast from pouty to fully porcupined, the hot fire of rage taking me by surprise. Get on this roller coaster, see where it flies off the track.

"What do I *care*? I'm your *mother*."

"That's never stopped you from letting me do whatever I wanted before."

"We're not having this conversation now."

"Oh yeah? Were we going to have this conversation, like, ever? I'm not like you." I'm shouting now, the words coming out of the ragged hole in my chest I've been filling with strangers and too many drinks, but now that I'm reaching into the mess there's no stopping me. "I'm not like you," I snarl again. "I'm not going to write Aurora off. Everyone else in her fucking life has abandoned her. She's down there on her own and she needs me and I'm going to get her."

Cass is staring at me like I've hit her. "I love Aurora. You know that."

"Not enough to pay attention! Not enough to stop her from practically killing herself! You left her in that house with Maia, you never even tried to take her with us—"

Cass cuts me off. Her voice is deadly. "I left that house because if I stayed there I knew I would be a junkie for the rest of my goddamn life. I left that house for *you*. To be a parent. To be the closest thing to a parent I knew how to be. I have always done everything I could for Aurora, but you were the first person I had to take care of. You. It's bad enough that you're out every night now, that I have no idea where you are half the time, that you spent this summer running around with a grown man on my watch. You are a child, do you understand? No matter what you think you are, you are still a child. You are not going to Los Angeles, and that's final."

"You're supposed to be the adult here! You're supposed to help her!"

"Listen. I was nineteen when I gave birth to you, and I knew I would have to look my own child in the face some-day and tell her I wasn't strong enough to stay sober while

I was pregnant, that I couldn't tell her who her father was because I didn't even know. I am doing the best I goddamn can, all right? And I might have made some mistakes with you, and god knows I made some mistakes with Maia, but if you think I am going to let you relearn every basic lesson I already have committed to memory you have got another think coming. You are not going to Los Angeles, you are not going after some musician" —she says *musician* like it's a bad word— "and you are not going to follow Aurora into whatever drugged-out hell she's headed for. You can't save her, baby. You can't. It's not your job." The muscles in her cheeks twitch. There's something she's not telling me. I think of what Maia said when I saw her after Aurora's party. *You tell Cass I said she can go to hell.*

"Why did we really leave Maia's?"

"I just told you."

"You didn't tell me the whole story. Why did you leave Aurora there? Why haven't you ever gone back? Why don't you and Maia talk?"

Cass actually flinches. "What did Maia tell you?"

"Nothing. She didn't tell me anything, because no one tells me a fucking thing. You're both supposed to be adults, and you act like fucking teenagers. You threw Aurora to the wolves and you won't even tell me *why.*"

She looks out the window. Fat raindrops spatter against the glass. The sky is a dull, sullen grey. "I almost killed you," she says quietly. Her eyes have a bright shimmer of unshed tears. "I almost killed you both. It was after Aurora's dad died. Things were . . . bad. I was loaded all the time. There were always people around with more drugs. This scary old guy."

"Minos."

She shakes her head. "I don't remember his name. He was always telling us things. We would see a world we didn't even know existed. We would be rich. We would be famous. He was right. Aurora's dad did get famous. And then everything went to shit. I can't explain to you what it was like. We were so sad, and it was impossible to say no to something that felt that good. You and Aurora didn't always—we didn't always—" She's crying for real now. "We didn't always take care of you. I don't know how much you remember. There was one day when I wanted to give the two of you a bath. You know how big that bathtub is in Aurora's room. Maia came in when I was—I was out. Passed out. You were both in the water. Aurora was under—" She makes a low, awful noise and stops, her shoulders heaving. I wait. "She would have drowned if Maia hadn't found us. Maia said a lot of things to me that I deserved. That no matter how fucked up she got she would never put either of you in danger. That she always made sure someone was around who could take care of you. It was true back then. You had a nanny. Aurora's dad's bandmates. There were a few people who were sober most of the time." She laughs, bitter. "I mean, there was a fucking *bodyguard* for a while. It was crazy. We were kids. It was so much money. We had no idea what we were doing. Maia told me to get out of her house before I killed her daughter, so I took you and I left. I knew I had to get sober. It took everything I had. By the time I was clean and realized how bad things had gotten over there, it was too late."

"What do you mean, it was too late? Why didn't you do something?"

"I told Aurora she could come live with us. She said she didn't want to."

"When was this?"

"Five or six years ago."

"Jesus, Cass! She was *twelve*. Of course she didn't want to come stay with us!"

"I don't always know what to do," Cass whispers. "I don't always do the right thing."

"Yeah," I say. "No shit."

"I loved Maia," she says. "I loved her. You can't imagine how much I loved her."

I think of Cass, reading her tarot cards every morning. *I was asking about Maia. It never changes much.* Not asking if Maia would ever get better. Asking if Maia would ever forgive her. So like Cass to leave it up to a deck of cards instead of going up to Maia's house and asking herself.

"You have no idea what it was like," Cass says. "All of those people. When I got sober, they acted like I had died. They stopped talking to me. Like I'd been erased. Maia was my best friend, and she wouldn't even let me in her house."

We're silent after that. I put the knife down. "Dinner's ready," she says finally. "Why don't you set the table?"

"I don't think I'm hungry." Before she can answer, I go into my room and shut the door.

That night I dream about the forest again. The bare trees clack as if a breeze has caught them, but the air is still. I stand in the same place I always stand, the black river inches from my bare feet, its surface sheened with a nacreous glow. I am looking for something, but I don't know what it is. I try to turn away from the river and run back down the path, but my feet are rooted to the earth. In this dream I can see the far bank.

On the other side of the river, Jack steps out of the trees. I can't make out the details of his face. His naked body is gaunt. Even from here I can see the stark lines of his ribs. "You came," he says, and then he repeats it, and this time it's Aurora's voice coming out of his mouth. I try to answer, but my mouth will not move. "You came," he says a third time, and his hair grows longer and turns white, his body changing, softening into Aurora's, and they are moving toward me, toward the river, and I want to warn them not to cross the water, tell them to stop, to stay there where it's safe, but I cannot speak. Blood pools beneath my bare feet. Jack takes one more step toward me, puts one foot in the river, and vanishes without a sound.

I wake up in the dark, gasping, touching my face, putting my fingers in my mouth and working my jaw. I whisper their names aloud in the dark, then reach over and turn on the light. Something in the room has changed, but I don't know what it is. I sit up in my bed, pulling the blanket tight around my shoulders. The curtains stir slightly and then still, as though a breeze has moved across them, but the window's shut tight. My closet door is open, my clothes hanging tidily. The slanted top of my drafting table is clean and bare. Crate of records, stereo, candles, lamp. Everything is where it should be. And then I see it. Aurora's and my map has changed.

It's not possible, but it's true. I get out of bed and walk over to the wall. There, tiny but perfectly rendered, is a tall clean-lined house at the edge of a river, with a forest at its back. The river is as black as it is in my dreams, and I think I can see the shiver of a current running through it. Aurora and Jack are standing in front of the house, their backs to the water and to me, their hands clasped. I touch the drawing. Nothing happens. The wall is cool and smooth. "Aurora," I whisper, and I think for one unreal second that I see the penciled lines of her head move, as though she's tilting one ear to listen. I look for a long time, but the drawing does not change again.

In the morning I dump my textbooks out of my old army backpack and throw in a clean pair of jeans. Socks, underwear. A T-shirt. My toothbrush. My sketchbook. Brushes and ink and pens. My tarot deck. I add my running shoes and then take them out again. Probably won't be jogging much where I'm going. Too bad. I hear they're big on fitness in LA. I tuck one of Cass's crystals in the front pocket of my jeans for luck. Cass is gone, but she's made coffee and left me a note. *I'm sorry. I love you. Mom.* I fold it and put it in my other pocket, next to the poster. I take down the biscuit tin from the shelf in the kitchen where she keeps a baggie of dried-out, ancient weed and a stash of emergency cash. I count the bills. Fifty-six dollars in tens and ones. Enough for a bus ticket. I won't have to hitch. I pick up the phone and dial Raoul, blowing on my coffee to cool it, poking through the refrigerator for something that looks like breakfast. When he answers, his voice is sleepy, and I can hear someone talking in the room behind him.

"Raoul? I need a favor. I was wondering if you could give me a ride to the bus station." He clears his throat, says something to the person who's with him. It's muffled, as though he's put one hand over the receiver. Then I hear him sigh.

"Where are you?" he asks.

I wait outside for Raoul's Volvo, smoking cigarettes on the front stoop of my building until he pulls up and I climb in. Rosaries dangle from the rearview mirror and there's a plastic statue of Jesus glued to the dashboard. The Jesus has a head that bobs as you drive and a slight walleye. The car smells like incense and pot, Raoul smells. He's wearing fingerless leather gloves with studs at the knuckles. "Nice," I say, petting them. I sit in his passenger seat while the engine idles, backpack in my lap, heater blasting in my face, and hand Raoul the poster. He unfolds it and smoothes it against the steering wheel. "Aha. And your mother cannot give you a ride to the bus station because?"

"Because she doesn't know."

"I had a feeling." He steeples his slender fingers and rests his forehead on them. "Will you tell her?"

"When I'm there."

"You're supposed to be in school?"

"Technically, yeah."

"Do you want a ride?"

"To *Los Angeles*?"

"Isn't that where you're going?" I look at him, his jet fall of hair, his generous mouth, his brown eyes smiling, and think that there is probably no one else in the world who is as blessed as I am. He's totally serious, unblinking. He would do it. He would do it, for me, because he's my friend.

"Oh, Raoul. I think that's technically, like, kidnapping. Transporting a minor across state lines. Like if we got pulled over you would be arrested." He shrugs. "No," I say. "I can take the bus. But thank you."

"Where will you stay? How are you getting them back here?"

"I haven't really thought that far ahead."

His sigh comes from somewhere in his toes. He rubs his forehead with the side of his thumb. "Okay," he says. "You know what? Don't tell me anything else." I take the poster from him and put it back in my pocket.

I try to memorize the streets as they flash by, the broad expanse of the bay, the exact shade of Doug firs in the changing light of late fall, the salt tang of the air. Heavy clouds edged in gold where the sun's creeping through. The far curtain of rain falling over the peninsula. Like if I can carry home with me it will keep me safe. We wind through the damp streets. Mia Zapata's scratchy, gorgeous voice howls from the speakers but it's too early for punk. I pop out the tape without asking, put in another one labeled "Nighttime" in sloppy Sharpied letters. It's Jeff Buckley. Sending me straight back to that night at Jack's when I read his tarot cards. The memory is so strong I push my hands through my hair, look out the window. *Not now.* "Who was at your apartment?" I ask, and Raoul smiles.

"Those fish-stall boys. Not as straight as you'd think."

"Oh my god. Which *one*?"

But he draws two fingers across his mouth like a zipper and shakes his head. "A gentleman never tells."

"I'll put you on the rack. I'll draw and quarter you. The tall one? The one who always wears that red knit hat?" He gives me a smug little smile and refuses to yield for the rest of the ride.

Raoul stops the car in front of the bus station down-town. He reaches over me and rustles around in the glove box, digs out a piece of paper and a pen and writes some-thing down before folding it in half and handing it to me.

"What's this?"

"My phone number."

"Raoul. I call you sixteen times a week. I know your phone number."

"Humor me?"

"Okay." I tuck the paper in my pocket next to the poster. "I owe you," I add, my hand on the door. "Again. Like, for-ever."

"Wait," he says. He takes off the wooden rosary he al-ways wears, loops it over my head next to Cass's amulet. "For luck."

"Raoul. I can't take this."

"It's a loan. Keep it safe and bring it back."

He hugs me tight. I hug him back, so fierce I can feel the whoosh of air leaving his lungs, and he makes a sur-prised noise. I squeeze my eyes shut, hang on for dear life. "I mean it." His voice is muffled. "Come back."

"I promise."

"No matter what."

"Okay."

He lets me go and I step out into the cold morning air. He leans across the seat. "No matter what. Call me if you need anything. I'll come get you. Okay?"

"Who will take care of Oscar Wilde if you have to drive to California?"

"Oscar Wilde loves the car. I'll buy him driving goggles. Be safe." I nod and shut the car door, hitch my backpack straps on my shoulders, take a deep breath. Raoul doesn't drive away until I'm inside.

At the counter I buy a ticket on the next bus to LA. When I reach into my coat pocket for my wallet there's a crackle, and I take out a wad of bills. Raoul slipped me nearly fifty dollars when he was hugging me. Fifty dollars he doesn't have to give away. I contemplate running after his car, but he'll be long gone by now. "Are you all right?" asks the lady at the counter. "Miss?" I'm crying again.

"Something in my eye."

"Uh-huh," she says, bored now. She was hoping for histrionics or confessions. A jilting. I'm sorry I can't humor her. "Your bus leaves in an hour and a half."

I take out my sketchbook, but I'm too antsy to draw. I pace around the station, buy a cup of coffee, drink it, buy another one, smoke, pace some more. I think about how long I have until Cass figures out I'm gone, what she'll do. It was shitty of me not to leave her a note, but the longer it takes her to realize what I've done, the more likely it is I'll make it to LA. She'll know where I went as soon as she figures out I'm gone, and all she would have to do is call the bus company to get me taken off at the next stop. I'll call her when I'm there, tell her I'm okay. Tell her I'm coming home. As soon as I have them. I refuse to think about what will happen if I can't find them. If Aurora isn't with Jack. If either of them tells me to go home. *I'm not this tough for nothing.* I stare down at my booted feet, turn up the collar of my leather jacket. If I tell myself how tough I am enough times, surely it will be at least a little bit true.

At last I shuffle aboard the bus, consoling myself with the thought that I'm far and away the least desperate-looking person boarding. A guy in a dirty white T-shirt, bare-armed despite the cold, sits next to me and asks where I'm from. When he opens his mouth I can see he's missing most of his teeth, and the remnants of a nasty bruise are fading from one cheek. Before I can answer, he tells me he's just gotten out of jail and is on his way home to see his woman. I nod, get out my headphones, hold them where he can see them, but he keeps talking. "You like to get high?" he asks.

"No thanks."

"I got good stuff. The best."

"Really. No thanks." I make a show of putting my headphones on, choosing music.

"You like to fuck?" I hear him say, and then I turn up the volume and look out the window. I can see his reflection in the glass. His lips are still moving.

The bus ride is like a fever dream. I can't sleep for more than a few minutes at a time. Sometimes the bus stops and we stumble out, smoke cigarettes by the side of the road in the cold air. Night falls. My seatmate gives up on me and moves on to some poor girl at the back of the bus, with more success. I can hear their soft grunts in the intervals between songs. I'm strung out on no sleep and nerves. I buy a cup of shitty gas-station coffee and a package of Pop-Tarts at the next stop. The sugar and caffeine don't make me any calmer. Cass will have figured out I'm gone by now, and every time the bus stops I chew on my nails, sure it's the cops. But it never is. When the bus rolls into Los Angeles, I can breathe again. It's Halloween morning, and I am going to find them, and everything is going to be fine.

———

This far south, the ocean seems like a different creature altogether from the moody grey monster I know at home. Gem-colored waves roll across the white-sand beach. Even this late in the year it's full of people sunbathing or playing volleyball. Ponytailed girls rollerblade past me on a boardwalk that stretches as far as I can see in either direction. Condominiums edge the beach, and I can see women basking on their balconies in neon bikinis. I can't remember the last time I ate. I buy a hot dog at a cart and walk down to the edge of the water.

I watch bodysurfers paddle out into the turquoise waves. Down the beach a boy is flying a kite, and a man is anointing his tanned, muscled body with oil.

"Read your palm?" someone says, and I look up. Blue-eyed surfer, straight out of a magazine. Shirtless, bronzed muscles, long blond hair, puka beads.

"Is that your line?"

"Line of work." He sits down next to me. "You look like a girl who needs answers."

What the hell. "How much?"

"Five bucks."

"Seriously?"

"Can't make a living selling weed alone."

I roll my eyes, take one of Raoul's bills out of my pocket, and hand it over. He pockets the five and takes my hand. His fingers are calloused and warm.

"Look at you," he says. "Wow."

"You tell that to all the girls?"

"Nope. You see this line?" He traces a long crease that crosses my palm. "This is some gnarly shit, girl. Serious destiny."

"Serious destiny," I mutter, mimicking his surfer's drawl.

"Oh, girl. Who did you piss off? You doing battle with some dark forces or something? This line says your life is about something way bigger than you." I scowl. Whatever, that's a thing you could say to anyone. Make them feel important. "This one," he continues, touching a different line now, "this is love. You got it bad for someone, right? Follow them to the ends of the earth, that kind of thing? This is a strong palm, sister. A strong, strong palm."

"I'm not your sister."

"You want me to read your palm or not?"

"Sorry."

"You're determined, right? You have a lot of anger. A lot of strength. But maybe too pigheaded. You have to learn to apologize."

"*I* have to learn to apologize?"

"You get in a fight with someone you love? Maybe it's your fault, maybe it isn't. Is it worth it to lose someone over the details? You are someone who has trouble letting go. You know that thing they say. Love something, set it free, it comes back to you maybe, maybe it goes for a trip. Outside your purview, sister."

I stare at him. He's serious. He's also totally stoned.

"What am I supposed to do?" I ask him.

"Come on, girl. I can't tell you that. I can only tell you what it says here. Something about a dad, right? You looking for a dad?"

"I don't have a dad."

"Doesn't mean you're not looking for one. But I think you'll be fine. Also, this line here? This one means you have stomach problems. You need to eat more yellow vegetables."

"Yellow *what*?"

"You know. Like squash. Butternut. Spaghetti squash is good, too. Has to be vegetables, though. Bananas won't work." He gives my hand a squeeze and gets to his feet. "Here," he says. "My compliments." He produces a joint out of nowhere and tucks it behind my ear. "Good luck, sister." I'm still staring as he saunters away down the beach.

The sun is warm on my back. I squirm out of my leather jacket and take out my sketchbook, draw the boy, the kite, the sunbathing man—who's stretched out now on a towel, glistening like a rotisserie chicken—the edges of the waves. Water is hard to draw, like any malleable thing, fickle in its lines and shadows. I think I'm catching it, but when I look at the page I've made it insipid and life-less. Stupid. High school. It's hardest when what I want to put on the page is so much bigger than what I'm capable of, when I know how it should look but not how to make it that way, because I'm nowhere near as good as I need to be.

I turn the page and draw a beer bottle sticking out of the sand, a dead crab, an empty shell. I draw for hours, until the sky blazes around the sinking sun in a gory, gorgeous mess like ink blowing out of a tattoo. I remember reading somewhere that pollution makes for better sunsets. I haven't eaten since the hot dog, who knows how many hours earlier. I stand up, my legs creaking in protest. I have to pee, and I'm so hungry I can barely walk. I give the surf-er's joint to a homeless guy with a baseball cap upended in front of him on the sidewalk. "Hey, thanks," he says, sur-prised.

I walk away from the beach, with its fancy glass-fronted restaurants, elegant people inside sipping wine from goblet-sized glasses and daintily forking a bite or two of salad into their mouths before pushing their plates away. All the women here look hungry. I see a divey Mexican restaurant wedged between two clothing boutiques. It's well lit and noisy, and even from the sidewalk I can smell the siren scent of cumin and fryer grease.

I order cheese enchiladas, and they come on a platter half the size of my table, swimming in mole sauce. The lady at the cash register brings me chips and guacamole and an apple soda in a glass bottle. I don't think there's any way I can fit all that food in my belly but I do it, scooping up mole and avocado with my chips and wolfing down the enchiladas. I watch the families around me, children running amok between the tables and begging scraps off their parents' plates when they've polished their own clean. No one looks at me. The restaurant is so normal, so cheerful, so full of people and light and chatter. When I finish eating I show the cashier the poster. "Is that near here?" I ask her, pointing to the club's address.

She looks at me for a while before she draws me a map on a paper napkin. "Not too far. Be careful there." I ask her what she means. She touches Raoul's rosary where it peeks out from my collar. "Be sure you take this with you."

Minos's club is near the water. I can't see the ocean, but I can smell it, and the air here is lighter. The club is a big, windowless building at the end of a dead-end block. The other buildings on the street are lifeless and dull: another warehouse, a shabby cinderblock building with a dirty white sign that reads ORTIZ'S MEATS. There's an alleyway cluttered with Dumpsters, next to an empty lot full of scraggly weeds and ringed in chain-link fence topped with razor wire. So this is what rich people go for. Real authentic.

Outside Minos's club, the street is alive. Sleek black cars disgorge sparkling women and men clad in leather and metal, spiked collars at their throats and spurs on their pointy-toed boots. Across the street, I lean against a wall and pull my hood up around my ears, watching as the squat building swallows skinny, sad-eyed girls with their hair spiked into Mohawks, skeleton charms dangling from their tiny wrists. Many of them are in costume: gossamer-wrapped fairies whose naked bodies are clearly outlined underneath yards of sequins and tulle; gore-spattered zombies draped in bandages; ghouls in sleek white, knotty hair hanging to their waists. I catch a glimpse of furred haunch and lean forward. It's the goat-limbed man from the roof-top party, wearing a feathered mask. He stops as if he can feel my eyes on him and turns, searching the darkness. I shrink back into the shadows and turn my face away, hoping the alleyway is enough to hide me. Finally he goes into the club. Some of the girls could be the blood-covered dancers I saw at the penthouse party. I thumb Raoul's rosary and shiver.

I wait until the flood of people slows to a trickle. At first I think there's no sign, but when I get closer I see that ERE-BUS is painted in neat red letters on the door. There's a bored-looking guy in sunglasses and a knit hat leaning against the wall. He's casual, slouching, but I can tell under the facade he's paying attention.

I knot my fists in the sleeves of my hoodie and walk up to the door. The bouncer looks me over without expression, looks away. "Not your kind of place."

"My friend is playing."

"You don't have friends here."

"I have to go in there," I say. "You don't understand." He's already waving forward the people behind me, holding aside the velvet rope to let them in. I chew the inside of my lip in frustration. He's too big for me to get past him. I take out the wad of Raoul's money and offer it to him. "Look, little girl," he says. "Go back to Kansas." I can feel the lump of Cass's quartz in my pocket, digging into my thigh.

"I have to get in there," I say again.

"I don't care what you think you have to do. I'm not letting you past this door, and in a minute I'm going to get angry with you. You don't want to see that."

I open my mouth again to protest, and then there's a noise like dead leaves rustling and Minos is standing behind the bouncer. Dressed in black, like always. *Like me,* I think suddenly. His flat eyes watch me. I have nothing to lose but the people I love most.

"You know why I'm here," I say to him. "Let me in." He lifts one shoulder, drops it. The same shrug he gave me in Aurora's bedroom. He points two fingers at me, curls them toward himself.

"Looks like Kansas grew up fast," the bouncer says. I shoulder past him and follow Minos into the huge warehouse. The inside of the building seems bigger than the outside. I can't see the ceiling, or any of the far walls. The air is so hot and thick with cigarette smoke and the stink of bodies I nearly gag.

"Where are they?" I shout after him, but he doesn't turn or answer. He doesn't look like he's moving any faster than a tall man walking, but I have to run to keep up with him and he still draws ahead of me. Minos vanishes into the swirl of grey, his black coat flapping behind him. Who wears coats like that in California? *Goddammit, Aurora,* I think. *You have the worst taste.* I trip over my own feet, stumble into a woman dressed like a storybook witch: long black dress and straggly black hair, wrinkled face, terrible eyes. She puts out one red-streaked hand and pushes me away. Her fingers leave wet red prints on my skin. A man with goat horns peeking out of his dark curls leers at me and sidles closer, running a hot hand down my leg. Disgusted, I push into the crowd to get away from him, men and women turning to look at me as I jostle through. The heat is overwhelming. *Get out of here get out of here get the hell out of here.* But I can't go until I've found them. A light flares to life on a makeshift stage across the room and a harsh, ugly cheer rises up from the crowd. I fight my way to the front, kicking at women in silk and fur. Disapproving snarls snake past me. The mass of bodies presses me up against the edge of the stage.

Jack stumbles onto the stage, and the crowd goes mad. I cling to the stage and hold on for dear life. If I lose my place it seems entirely possible I'll be torn to pieces. Behind me an awful howl rises and bodies surge forward. I stare up at Jack, willing him to look down at me, but he gazes out unseeing over the seething mass of people. He looks terrible, his face gaunt, his back bent under the weight of the guitar slung around his neck like an anvil. *"Jack,"* shouts the crowd behind me, *"Jack, Jack, Jack,"* one name rising from hundreds of throats, pounding into the hot dark like the beat of a drum. He opens his mouth but makes no sound, and all the *Jacks* run together into a blur of noise. I cover my ears with my hands and cower. He strikes a chord, and the frenzy behind me grows even wilder.

This time when he plays it's the song of someone who's dying. I weep as I watch him, his body jerking as though his limbs are being pulled by invisible strings, his mouth open and working, his eyes with that empty, terrible stare. The air around him fills with hundreds of huge-winged dark moths that flutter out into the darkness. I throw my hands up to protect my face from heavy, soft wings that leave thick traces of something powdery and terrible smelling across my arms. There is no joy in what he plays, only an immense, terrible pain. I can see a dry wasteland stretching out under a starless sky. Behind me someone screams above the rest of the noise, and the air fills with the metallic scent of blood. I kick back behind me again, fighting to keep from being crushed against the stage. When I punch into the knot of bodies my hand comes back slick with gore. Still Jack plays, a single chord that grates and wails into the hot dark. Something knocks me into the stage and I hit my leg hard, Cass's quartz grinding into the soft part of my thigh; but instead of pain, a soft coolness spreads from where the stone struck me. I shove one hand into my pocket and close my fingers around the crystal. The noise around me dims and I can breathe more easily. I close my eyes and imagine Cass, standing over the stove, stirring tofu with a wooden spoon. The ordinariness of the image eases my terror.

At last the song ends. I open my eyes. Jack's sunk to his knees. I am almost close enough to him to touch him. "Jack! *Jack!*" He doesn't hear me. He bows his head, but not before I catch a glimpse of his expression. Desperate, hunted. He looks terrified. The roar behind me is so immense it has mass, like a vast flock of some nightmarish bird rising into the dark. With a visible effort, Jack stands, listing as if he's drunk, staring at nothing. There's a movement in the darkness, and then Minos is striding onto the stage, moving toward Jack, catching him even as he slumps back toward the ground. Holding him up with bony fingers, the bony face triumphant, the hollow eyes full of fire. Behind me the crowd gets even louder, the massive shriek battering at me hard as a fist.

Minos tugs Jack closer, bends his head down in an awful kiss. I can't bear to watch. I turn my head away, bury my face in my own sweat-soaked shoulder. The crowd turns on itself, frenzied and gleeful. Some of the screams seem more particular, more gruesome. Hands grab at me, tear at my hair. When I look up again Jack and Minos are gone. All the rage I have ever felt in my short angry life flares up in me now, a white pulse that strips all the fear from me. I am going to find them and then I am going to get out of here. There's a door to the left of the stage, and maybe this is hell but I bet it still works the way a club works. I fight my way through, kicking and biting, pulling hair, punching, until I'm standing in front of the doorway. "Minos!" I shout into the dark. "Goddammit!" I scream his name over and over again, but I'm still surprised when the darkness yields him up and he's standing in front of me.

"I want to see him," I say. "You have to let me see him." I push past him. I'm in a hallway, like I thought. Not so much worse than some of the clubs I've been in. I stumble down the hall, past closed doors, a reeking horror that is maybe a bathroom, and then I see it: a door that's open a crack. I walk through it without knocking. Jack is there, his back to me. His shoulders are slumped, but he's standing.

"Jack." He whirls around. His face when he sees me is equal parts horror and, I am delighted to see, joy.

"What are you *doing* here?" he asks, but I'm already running at him, flinging myself into his arms. He grunts, startled, but holds me tight. "You crazy thing," he says. "You crazy, crazy thing. You should never have come here."

"I missed you," I say, "so much. I missed you so much."

"I missed you, too," he says, and then he kisses me. Out of all the kisses, ever, it is the best one. A kiss that is *sorry* and *I love you, get me out of here* and *forgive me*. A kiss that is the two of us driving west, getting free of here, going all the way to where the ocean meets the sky. A kiss that is all the time before any of this happened, that brief window of joy when we were just two people holding hands in a starlit park. A kiss like Jack's music. Finally we break apart, gasping. I can hardly breathe.

"Come home with me," I manage. "I came for you."

"Sweet thing." His eyes are so sad.

"I mean it."

"I know you mean it. I can't."

"I was wrong. What I said to you when you left. I didn't get it."

"I know."

"But I get it now. And you did what you wanted. And now you can come home."

"Look at me," he says gently, and I look at him. That face. So beautiful, so tired. He looks years older than he did the last time I saw him. "I can't go home. That's not how it works. I came here to do this. I have to see it through."

"He'll kill you."

"Maybe. But I don't think so."

"Jack."

"This is all I've ever wanted," he says. "Not being famous. I don't care about being famous. That's where Aurora's dad and I are different. That's what killed him. He thought he wanted it, and then he got it, and he didn't realize until it was too late that no one wants that, not really. But me—do you have any idea what it's like to play for them?"

"I saw you. I saw your face on that stage."

"I didn't say it was easy."

"But I came to get you."

"You didn't come for me," he says. "Look me in the face and tell me you came for me."

"I did—" I begin, and then I stop. He's right. He's been right, this whole time.

"This is what I want," he says. "Let me go. Find her. She needs you."

"I love you," I say, and this time I say it loud, so he can hear. So he knows. *All the best artists are selfish.* He smiles, tilts my chin up. Kisses me again, a kiss that is softer, sadder. Goodbye.

"I love you, too." He reaches into his pocket. "Take this." He hands me his knife. "You'll need it, where you're going."

"But—"

"Take it."

"I'll give it back. Someday." *Someday soon,* I think, but I know better.

He looks at me. Dark eyes, dark hair, the pulse at his throat, the smell of his skin. The worn fabric of his shirt, his scuffed boots. Pebbles beneath me, the sound of waves. Wind in my hair. His hand in my hand. Ink on skin. The taste of peaches. The Fool. The Lovers. Death. I touch his wrist, his hip, underneath his shirt to feel the heat of his skin and the line of muscle there. Memorizing. *I will never love anyone like this again.* Hold the thought in my palm like a stone. Let it fall. He takes my hand from his waist, brings my knuckles to his mouth. Closes his eyes. We stand like that for a moment, and then he releases me.

"Tell me you are choosing this," I say. *Tell me you are choosing this over me.*

"I am choosing this. I chose this a long time ago."

I can't look at Jack anymore or I will fall apart. Minos waits behind us, watching.

"Minos," I say. "I want to see Aurora."

When he speaks at last his voice is in my head and not in the world, a voice as old and dry as dust. *You do not know what you are asking for, child.*

"Try me," I say. I look at Jack one last time. Drinking him in.

"I love you," he says again. "Now go."

I turn away from him and follow Minos into the dark.

There is no time in hell. We walk for what could be hours or days. It's still too hot, but the noise dies down and I'm alone with Minos and my own breath, the crunch of my footsteps on what I think is stone. We are in some kind of tunnel, heading down. The angle of the floor is steep enough in places to nearly trip me up. There is no light of any kind.

Minos is as silent as always, but something has changed, in the dark, between the two of us.

"Tell me who you are," I say after we have been walking for a long time. "I know there's someone there. Tell me who you are."

I was a king. In a different time. Now I am a gatekeeper.

"You collect people."

I collect beautiful things.

"For who?"

The nights are long, here. We're still walking. We'll be walking forever, I think, down and down and down. We'll be walking still when the world ends and the stars crash into the earth and the moon spins off through an empty sky. I think I am tired, I think I am tired beyond tired, but if I stop moving I won't start again, so I put one foot after the other, following him down. My throat is dry, sweat a salt crust on my skin. There's a blister puffing up on one heel. I lick cracked lips, cough, keep walking. If he thinks this is enough of a test, he has never met the likes of me before. I won't ask him how long it takes to get there. I will not let the terror of the dark get hold of me. If this is a test, I will fucking pass it. I will pass any test this creepy skeleton in a crappy suit can give me. Let them turn me into stone or water or flowers. I came here for my lover and the girl who is my sister, and they were mine before anyone else tried to take them from me, before this bony motherfucker showed up on my stoop and let loose all the old things better left at rest. Jack I will let go; Jack is on his own, now. But I will die before I leave Aurora down here. *Take your bacchanal, take your bloody-limbed girls, take your witches and your three-headed dog, and leave me and my love alone.* Down, down,

down, and further down. Every story I've ever heard about Minos's kind coming to life in my head. Persephone trapped in the underworld, Andromeda strapped to a rock. Medusa with her snaky head. The Fates, the harpies. Arachne cursed into a spider's body, forever spinning because she loved herself too well.

Why are you here? Why here, of all places, this city, this time? I wonder.

We are everywhere. The voice in my head is his. I didn't know he could hear me, could see inside.

"All I want is what's mine." My tongue is so dry I can hardly shape the words.

What belongs to you is not for you to decide, child.

"Yeah," I mutter. "That's what you think, asshole."

Far greater heroes than you have come under the earth and not returned.

"I'm not a hero," I say. "I'm a bitch."

And then I can feel it: The air is changing. We're coming out of the tunnel into the forest of bone trees. I know where we are. I've been here every night for months. The river is ahead. I can hear the dog howling. Bare white trees, thorny vines. Things moving between the branches. We do not walk long before the trees stop, the line of the wood's edge as sharp as if it has been cleaved away. We walk through the white trunks until we reach the place where they end and the river is in front of us. Minos stops.

If you cross this river, you will not return.

"People have."

Once. In all the history of time.

"I'll chance it." Shrug. I want to cut off his arm and feed it to him. I follow him to the edge of the water and stop.

The far bank is shrouded in darkness. He motions with one bony hand and a boat glides out of the darkness toward us, cowl-draped ferryman at the helm. There's no way out but through. Minos steps into the boat, surprisingly graceful for someone so tall, and offers me his hand. I laugh out loud, take it. Hold tight. Take the first step. The second. The boat doesn't rock. I'm in. I know you're supposed to pay the ferryman but I don't have any gold coins. I find Cass's crystal in my pocket, hand it over. The ferryman takes it, pale hand gleaming in the dark. I can't see his face under the brown hood. He makes a fist around the crystal, and then it's gone.

It takes a long time to cross the river. The water is thick as oil and I am careful to keep my hands inside the low edges of the boat. A dank fog rises off the water. Looking too hard at the current makes me dizzy. Instead I stare at my knees, the place where the fabric is fraying and I can see a patch of skin. I think of Jack's hand there, of kissing him over the tarot cards, of Aurora laughing, blowing smoke out my window, drinking Dr Pepper in my bed. I think of the most ordinary things I can imagine. Puppies, why not? The godawful still life I am working on in art class. Cass blowing her brown hair out of her eyes while she measures herbs. Raoul putting Oscar Wilde on my head, Raoul laughing, Raoul bringing me hot chocolate with chilies in it. I think of Jack, not the musician but the person who is barely not a boy, smiling at me with his joker's smile. Telling me to draw him pictures of kittens and sailboats, ridiculous things. Down here in the dark there is no light but the light I bring with me, and I will not fail. I will not fail. *Do you hear me, Aurora, I am coming for you. I am coming.*

I'm not the kind of girl they're looking for in hell. I'm not pretty; I don't play instruments; half the time I can barely draw. But I'm the girl they'll never forget, because I'm the girl who'll win.

At last I can make out the other side through the heavy dark. The ferryman poles the boat toward a smooth place where the bank flattens out. Dark sand, slick with the same oil that sheens the surface of the water. I catch one foot on the gunwale as I'm getting out, almost tip into the water, catch myself at the last minute, one hand inches from the surface. Something tells me I don't want to get wet. I can feel Minos's eyes on my back. "I'm fine," I say, to no one but myself. Minos is moving past me, not waiting. I have to half-run to keep up with him. But I remember how fast he moved in the warehouse. This time, for whatever reason, he is letting me follow.

We are standing on the edge of a vast bone-white plain that glows with an unholy light of its own under the empty sky. *So Death's great city welcomed armies of the dead.* But there are no armies here, only me and the hot blood in my human veins. Ahead of us stands a palace. There's no other word for it: looming, massive, rising out of the white rock like a tumor. Black stone walls, grease-shined like the river. I can see hundreds of doors all around it, and all of them are open. Locks don't matter, here. My stomach knots, and I can't catch my breath. This is more than anything I bargained for. This is not a place I should be, not a place anyone from my time or my world should ever have to see. Minos does not turn around, but he pauses. I can feel him, at the edges of my thoughts. Amused, contemptuous. His disdain kindles my courage. I take the first step forward, walk past him. I know where I'm going, now. He can follow me.

It takes longer than I think it should to cross the white plain and draw close to the nearest door. *Aurora,* I think, *Aurora, Aurora, Jack.* Holding their names under my tongue like talismans, I take the first step inside.

I am back in the penthouse apartment Aurora took me to. The room is empty and the chandeliers are unlit, the greasy candles melted into long strings of wax. Beyond the windows I see not the plain we crossed but the black ocean, the black sky of my dreams. It's colder here than anywhere I've ever been. I draw my sleeves over my knuckles, but it's no use. Nothing can keep out this chill. It slips between my ribs and down my throat. I shiver and tug at Raóul's rosary. I'm starting to wonder if I will spend the rest of my life in places that aren't entirely real, and then I think about where I am and how the rest of my life may not be a very long time at all, and then I decide to think about something else. Ripley. Thomas the Rhymer. *Weetzie Bat.* Plum sauce. Wendy Wanders. Raoul's tamales. Oscar Wilde. Cheetos. JD with his homemade bomb. Cow tipping. Staying frosty. Keith Richards. Keith Richards is definitely cooler than Minos. Maybe even older. I think about bringing this up, decide against it.

The room is smaller than I remember from the party. One wall is windowless, painted white and lined with oil paintings in simple frames. I walk closer, unable to help myself. Security guards at museums hate me; I'm forever trying to touch the art. These are a series of murky oil landscapes all done in a similar style. Each one is populated with tiny figures, their faces rendered in perfect detail. A man rolling a boulder up a hill, his shoulders covered in gore, his face full of pain. A man tied down, mouth open in a scream, while vultures tear open his belly. A line of sad-faced women trying to carry water in sieves. And people I know, too. People who lived too fast and died badly. When I find the picture of Aurora's father, I am not surprised. He's in the garden of Aurora's house, looking at something outside the frame of the painting. His face looks the same way it does in my memory. At the very edge of the picture, there's a half-obscured figure in a dress that might be Maia. Or Aurora.

"This is fucked," I say. I turn back to Minos, and then I see him. The tall pale man from the party, the one whose touch burned my skin. Minos's boss. I can't pretend anymore that I don't know who he is, don't know who the two people I love most in the world have been cutting bargains with. His ice-blue eyes are mocking. He's standing by the windows on the far side of the room, as casual as if we were all at a cocktail party. Aurora lies crumpled at his feet. *Please, let her be alive,* I think. *Please. Please.*

"Come forward," says the ice-eyed man. I can feel my shoulder burning where the thorns pierced my skin. I cross the room. Slow, slow steps. If Aurora is dead I don't want to know yet.

But she isn't: I can see that, when I'm standing in front of the god of hell. Faint rattle of breath in her throat, faint rise and fall of her chest. She's so beautiful now she is transcendent, as though passing over from the realm of the living stripped her of any remaining imperfection. I am so filled with love for her I can hardly talk. "I came here for her," I say.

"I know what you came here for," he says. "What will you give me for her?" The terrible eyes are amused.

Once there was a musician who fell in love with a girl. When she died too young he followed her into darkness, played so beautifully that even the lord of death was moved. *Take her,* he said to the musician, *and bring her to the world above. But if you falter on the path, she is ours forever.*

But I am not the musician, and I am not the girl. I am only myself, muscle and bone, stubborn and jealous and sometimes too mean, selfish and in love. I am only all the things that make me, and the best of those is her. I have nothing to offer the god of hell, no sweet-voiced song to trade, no unearthly beauty, no rare and precious gift. I can't charm animals or fight kings or sail a fleet of ships to a hundred monster-haunted islands, trick a Cyclops, make a goddess fall in love with me. I curl my hands into fists and stand there, helpless and out of luck. I don't even win at board games.

Draw for us, Minos says. That death's-head mask is as expressionless as ever. For the first time it occurs to me to wonder why he brought me here, why he shot me full of the same glimmering stuff that pulled Aurora down into the dark and then sent me home before I could cross all the way over. Why he led me down that long passage to this wretched palace of death. Why he's offering me good advice now, reminding me of the single thing I know how to do better than anyone else I know. The two of them are watching me, inscrutable.

Fine. Draw for them. That I can do. I sink to my haunches,

take out my brushes and ink. My sketchbook. I turn to a blank page. Breathe in. Start to draw. I draw me and Aurora, the story of us. I draw us as little girls, clasping our bloody palms together and making promises about forever. I draw us in the pit, clothes sticking to our bodies, our faces jubilant, waiting for the next chord. I draw us in the woods, sleeping under a canopy of leaves. I draw the map we made on the walls of my room, the world we swore we'd find together. I draw the wretched mess of my own envy, draw the poison I let creep into my heart, draw how much I wanted her broken fairy-tale life, how much I wanted her perfect face, her endless charm. I draw us in her bathtub, laughing at each other. I draw Aurora as Ripley, battling aliens in the far reaches of space; I draw her as Aphrodite rising out of the ocean; I draw her as the mermaid Ondine singing mortals down to the deep. I draw her as I know her: capricious, fierce, lovely, beloved. I draw Raoul and Oscar Wilde, Raoul and the fish-stall boys, Raoul bringing me back to what matters over and over again. I draw what it cost me to leave Jack standing in that terrible room, draw how much I hope he'll find what he's looking for, the future bright and hopeful still. I draw a way out, a way through. Draw the light of his music moving through me, that impossible gift, the music that started all of this, that drew these old gods to us like cats batting mice for sport. I draw Cass and her tarot cards, counting out the ways to keep from saying sorry; Maia kicking aside the life raft and plunging into the deep. Both of them letting us go too far until we got to here. I draw as though I'm drawing for my life, for Aurora's life, drawing us a way out of here, a way back to the world we lived in before, where everything was simpler and the only things that could hurt us were the things I already knew. I draw until my hands cramp into claws and my vision blurs and my fingers are black with ink. Sweat runs in stinging rivulets between my breasts. Aurora's chest rises and falls. I draw for hours or days or months or years, I draw until time stops meaning anything at all. I draw until Minos bends down and gently takes the brushes from me. He stands and faces the ice-eyed man.

Let them go. I wish it.

"Take her, then," says the god of hell. I can see eternity in his bored blue eyes, all the dusty centuries that have passed while he waited in this room for something to happen. No wonder he likes to fuck with people. We're the daytime soaps for him. *The Real World: Hades.* "Take her, and see how far you get, child."

I don't wait for them to change their minds. When I try to stand my legs buckle, and the pain in my knees makes me suck my breath in quick and sharp. Minos reaches out one bony hand but I shrug it away, struggle to my feet alone and stand there breathing hard until the room stops spinning.

"Aurora," I say. "We have to go." She doesn't stir. Nobody said this was going to be a free ride, but I wish I had at least a couple of crafty Fates on my side. I take a deep breath and pick Aurora up like I'm a newlywed carrying her across a threshold. One of her arms slung around my shoulder. Her white hair spilling down my back. She murmurs something and opens her eyes at last.

"Babycakes. You came."

"Let's get the fuck out of here," I say into Aurora's cheek. I carry her out of that room with my own two hands, and I do not look back.

The ferryman is waiting where we left him, silent in his dark boat. I heave Aurora's legs over the side, sit her in the front of the boat. Aurora slumps forward, and I climb over her. We sit like that, her nearly unconscious, me expectant, but the boat doesn't move. I rack my mind for fairy-tale passwords, but everything I know is out of Grimm's. "Open sesame" is probably a little *au courant* for these purists. I'm still freezing, and the empty night is not particularly cheering. Somewhere in the distance a dog howls, and I shudder. That thing, I do not want to see again.

I don't hear Minos, don't see him crossing the plain. One minute he isn't there and the next he is. *You have to pay the ferryman. Cross the river and follow the path. It will take you a long time. But I think you are stronger than you look.*

"Pay him what?" But Minos won't answer. "Why are you helping me?"

Minos steps forward and reaches over the gunwale, rests one hand on Aurora's forehead. He bends down and kisses her at the place where her dark roots meet her brow. *It has been a very long time. But once I, too, knew how to love.* He reaches into his black coat and hands me my sketchbook and brushes. *These are yours.*

"Thank you."

He shakes his head. *You will not thank me.* In his dead eyes there's something like a very human sorrow. He raises one hand, in farewell or in benediction, and then he is gone, nothing where he stood but the empty plain and the dark palace in the distance.

I have to pay the ferryman. Maybe the ferryman wants blood. But when I take Jack's knife out of my pocket, flip open the blade and press it against the thin pale skin at my wrist, the ferryman shakes his head. He leans forward, the hood still covering his face, and touches Aurora's hair.

"No way," I say. "That's not up to me. That's hers." I offer him Cass's amulet, Raoul's rosary—not that that's mine to give, either. The knife. My hoodie, my sketchbook, my boots. But he ignores me. "Goddammit," I mutter. "I'm sorry," I tell her. "It grows." I put Jack's knife to her hair and start to cut. The knife is sharp but too small for what I'm using it for, and Aurora has a lot of hair. Long moments pass as I saw away, hanks coming off in my hands. I cut my finger and yelp, put it in my mouth for a moment. When I go back to cutting the white of Aurora's hair is stained with my blood. At last I have a pile of pale strands, a larger mass than I would have thought possible. I offer it to the ferryman. "Rumpelstiltskin," I say, but if he gets the joke it doesn't register. These guys don't have much of a sense of humor.

The ferryman poles us back to the other shore. Maybe it's imagination or fear, but the crossing seems to take too long. The boat's sluggish, the current strong. I chew on my fingers and close my eyes. I can feel the palace pulsing behind me, tugging at me with some unsubtle force. *You will not thank me.*

The boat scrapes against sand at last. "I could use your help," I say to the ferryman, but he doesn't move. He has

Aurora's hair in his lap, stroking it as though it's a pet. It quivers like a living thing under his touch. I watch for a moment, fascinated, and then heave Aurora to her feet, careful not to rock the boat. To get her out I'll have to more or less throw her. "You have to help me," I say to her, shaking her. She lifts her head, opens her eyes. Looks right at me.

"I saw my dad." Her voice is clear and high.

"Aurora, you couldn't have. Your dad's dead."

"Everyone here is dead."

"Not you. And not me. Can you take a big step? Over the side?" She obeys. The boat tips madly as she steps out, and I think for a second I'll go flying, but I hop clear before I can lose my footing.

"He's going to teach me to play the guitar," she says happily. "Like Jack."

"Aurora. We have to walk now." Her eyes roll back in her head and her knees buckle. She tumbles forward into my arms, nearly sending me backward into the river. She's out cold. It wouldn't be hell if it was easy. "Piggyback it is," I tell her.

She's so light I barely notice her weight at first, as I move through the forest. But by the time I reach the tunnel my shoulders are beginning to hurt. I hitch her body up against my back, get my hands more firmly underneath her thighs, walk into that yawning mouth. Begin to climb.

If I thought the way down was long, it is nothing compared to the way back up. Aurora's limp body is a dead weight. My shoulders burn, my thighs ache, my calves knot. Sweat runs down my chest, drips from my forehead and into my eyes, but I can't move my arms to wipe it away without dropping her. I put my head down, think about putting one foot after the other. One step, one step, one more step. My throat is so dry I can't swallow, my lungs are on fire, my hands are cramping, one step, one step, one step. I have no idea how long I've been climbing or how long I have left. Pain travels up my spine and shuts down reason, shuts down everything but one step, the next step, the next step, the next. The walls of the tunnel closing in. Suffocating heat, darkness, silence. One step, one step, one step. My feet are wet, and I wonder dully if I stepped in the river after all, if the taint of that water is enough to keep me in this hallway forever, doomed like Sisyphus to carry my burden until the end of time. The darkness presses against me. I can feel raw fear rising in my chest and threatening to choke me, but if I stop now I will never start again. I close my eyes. It makes no difference. But there's something about the darkness behind my own lids that's strangely comforting. Cass's amulet burns against my chest. One step, one step, one step.

I am beyond hope, beyond light, so certain that I have moved into a world where I will be climbing forever that when the tunnel ends I walk smack into hot metal and stand for a moment, reeling, before I let Aurora's limp body slide down my back. When I try to move my hands the pain is so intense my knees buckle and I crash into the metal again. A long time passes before I can work my hand forward enough to touch the surface. To brush my fingers against something round and smooth, waist-height. Doorknob. I am standing at a door. It takes more than a few tries before I can close my hand around the knob, turn, push.

The flood of sunlight is so bright I turn my head away in

pain and behind me, in the tunnel, Aurora cries out. I totter there for a moment, leaning on the door, eyes screwed shut against the glare, until the green flash behind my lids seeps away and I dare to crack one eye open, still squinting. Concrete. Parked cars. A street. I am looking at a street. I am looking at the street in front of Minos's club. I take a step forward, shaky-legged as a toddler. Across the street, men are filing into Ortiz's Meats. Going to work. Like it's some kind of ordinary morning. I try to call out but my voice comes out as a croak. One of them turns, sees me, stares. Says something to another man and both of them walk toward me, cautious.

"Lady, what happened to you?" he says when he gets close enough for me to hear him. He's staring at my feet in horror. I follow his gaze. My boots are gone and my feet are covered in so much blood I can't see skin.

"My friend," I say, pointing behind me, and then a dark haze rises up and swallows me whole.

NOVEMBER

In my dream I am waiting in a white room at the end of a long corridor. For some reason I'm in bed. My feet hurt. The blanket is scratchy and the air smells wrong, like chemicals, and underneath the tang of pee. Aurora is standing over me. Too thin but still beautiful, her face haloed in short black hair tipped with white, her dark eyes huge and sad. I haven't seen her in a long time, but I can't remember why. I open my mouth to ask her why she cut her hair, but no sound comes out. She is talking, has been talking for a while maybe, or maybe not. Maybe we just got here. She is wearing a white sleeveless silk shirt that exposes the graceful line of her collarbone, and I am wearing some kind of blue dress, which is clearly not mine because I would never wear a dress if Aurora didn't make me, and it is made out of thin cheap cotton and I am naked underneath it and I want to know where my underwear is and what is going on, but this is a dream, so maybe that's why everything is weird. The light is watery and unfamiliar. Too sharp and pale. White around the edges like I am looking at everything through a lens. "I love you," Aurora is saying, "more than anything. But I miss him so much." I try to sit up, but there's a weight on my chest, a pile of stones I can't see pressing me down. I open my mouth but no sound comes out. She takes my hand and kisses my knuckles. "Don't be mad at me," she whispers. And then she's turning, walking away from me. I watch her back recede down the long, gleaming hall.

"Aurora," I say at last, but she's long gone.

When I wake up Raoul is the first thing I see and I am so confused I shut my eyes again, open them. But there he is, sitting in a metal chair upholstered in garish turquoise vinyl, reading *Optometry Today*. He is wearing tight black jeans and a white Depeche Mode shirt that is falling off him in artful tatters and a red beanie that looks as out of place on him as a collared shirt. The room I am in is exactly like the room in my dream.

"I didn't know you were interested in vision," I say. The words come out thickly. My throat is a desert. My mouth tastes like something died in it. He looks up and a slow smile spreads across his face.

"You better not be alluding to my earthy indigenous spirituality," he says. "Or else I might make you regret your return to the world of the living."

"What," I say, not so much a question but an irritated protest. There's a tube coming out of my arm and the pee smell is real, although as far as I can tell it isn't coming from me. The blue dress is real, too, and I can feel that it's open at the back because the sheets are scratchy against my bare skin, and I remember where they have dresses like this. It's not a dress. I am wearing a smock. "Holy shit. Am I in a hospital? How did I get in a hospital?" I try to sit up, and pain shoots through my entire body. "Fuck!" I yell.

"That's my girl," Raoul says. "Do you remember anything?"

"I remember—I got on the bus—" I stop and think. Raoul took me to the bus. I got on the bus to find Aurora. I got off the bus and ate a hot dog. I went to hell. I cut off Aurora's hair. "I ate a hot dog," I tell him.

"Not recently, you didn't."

"I ate a hot dog this morning. This afternoon. Maybe yesterday. I had some enchiladas. Last night. What day is it?"

Raoul's expression is unreadable. "The day after Halloween. A factory worker found you passed out on the sidewalk in front of an abandoned building and called 911 this morning. When they brought you in you were dehydrated and starving and you had pretty much no skin left on your feet. Any of this ring a bell?"

Ortiz's Meats. "It wasn't an abandoned building. It was a club."

"I'm telling you what the doctor told me."

Something he told me is wrong and I think about what it is. "Wait. How am I starving? I ate today. Yesterday. Recently."

"The doctor said you hadn't eaten anything for at least five or six days."

"Raoul, that's impossible, you know that. You *saw* me yesterday. The day before yesterday. I mean, I don't think I ate breakfast—"

"I'm telling you what the doctor told me," he says again. "She asked me if you had spent the last week walking here barefoot from Mexico and I said I didn't think so but that you were a pretty unpredictable kind of person."

I ignore this. "How did you get here?"

"They found my phone number in your pocket and called me when you were admitted."

"Oh shit, my mom—"

"Is trying to get Aurora's mom on a plane. She's pretty pissed, so I'd spend the next few hours composing a very comprehensive apology."

"Cass went up to Maia's?"

"I guess so."

"So it's, like, a big deal that I ran away."

"Yes. A very big deal."

"Oh."

"A *very* comprehensive apology."

"I brought your rosary back."

"I know."

"Can I see Aurora? Is she awake?"

Raoul pauses. "Aurora isn't here."

"She's in a different hospital?"

"You were alone when they found you."

I stare at him, my mouth open. "Raoul. She was with me. I went down there and I got her. I brought her back. She was here. In the hospital. I thought it was a dream, but she was here. We could find her. That couldn't have been that long ago, when I saw her. She didn't mean—she couldn't have meant to leave. I carried her. I carried her the whole way."

Raoul doesn't say anything. He watches whatever is moving across my face now, and when I start to cry for what feels like the thousandth time in a month he takes my hand and kisses my knuckles, the way Aurora did, and holds my fist, there, against his mouth, the way Jack used to. I cry for me, for her, for Jack, for Cass and Maia. For her dad. For all of us. For how stupid I was, down there in the dark, thinking my own love was enough to trump the past. They didn't stop me from leaving because it had never been me they wanted anyway. Because they knew she was already theirs. *You will not thank me.* When I'm done crying I sit for a long time, holding Raoul's hand and hiccupping. "That fucking bitch," I whisper. But I don't mean it, and he knows it. The whole of my life stretches out in front of me, the life that is starting now, the life that does not have Aurora in it, and I turn my face away from the emptiness before I start crying again.

"What was the point? What was the point of going after her?"

"What is ever the point of love?" I shake my head. He smiles, a smile with so much sadness in it I don't know where to look. "You did good," he says. He takes something out of his pocket and hands it to me. The soft leather is familiar. Cass's amulet. They must have taken it off when I got here. I loop the cord around my neck again and stare at it.

"So much for that," I say.

"You're here," he says. "You're alive. You went there and you came back." If I look at him I will cry more and I am so tired of crying, tired of myself, tired of my own stupid hope-filled heart. I touch his beanie.

"I knew it was the one with the red hat."

"Well, obviously," he says. "I wouldn't settle for less."

"Can you hand me the remote control," I say, and he does.

When Cass comes there is a lot of shouting. "What the *fuck* were you thinking," she yells, over and over again, until one of the nurses comes in and coldly tells her if she doesn't calm down she will have to leave. Maia is a trembling wraith in Cass's wake, wobbly but, as far as I can tell, sober. They won't look at each other. I can't even imagine what the plane ride was like. They probably sat in separate aisles. Cass subsides at last, explains to me in a low voice the numerous ways in which I have fucked up. I can feel my heart coming apart in my chest. *Aurora. Aurora.*

"You're one to talk," I say, when I can't take it anymore. Cass stops short. Maia sits on the edge of my bed and takes my hand.

"You saw her." I nod. "I did a really bad job." I nod again. She looks at Cass and snorts softly through her nose. "You were always the lucky one," she says without rancor. "You could take and take and it always worked out for you."

"You had everything," Cass says. "Everything. You had love. You had money. You had a home."

"You have a daughter," Maia says. Cass winces.

"So do you," I say.

"I'm sorry," Maia says. "For what it's worth. You have no idea how sorry I am."

Cass sits next to Maia and puts a chin on her shoulder. Maia starts but doesn't push her away. They look down at me, sad and solemn. I wonder if Aurora and I look like that; if we'll look like them when we're the same age, our eyes full of stories, lines at the corners, grey in our hair. They loved each other once, and then they fucked it up, and now here I am fucking it up again. Whether any of us gets a second chance is anybody's guess. *Aurora, why'd you leave me here with the two of them*, I think. *Aurora. Come back. Come home.*

I turn my face to the wall, close my eyes. "I think she should rest," Raoul says. "We can talk later." Maia and Cass stand up. Raoul touches my shoulder, leans forward to kiss my hair. "Don't forget," he murmurs, too low for Cass and Maia to hear. "You are still loved. You are anchored here by love." I cover his hand with mine and sink back into sleep.

In my dream the three of us are sitting at the edge of the black river. Aurora is skipping stones. Jack has his guitar, strums quietly. The bone trees clack behind us. The dog howls. We're alone. No Minos, no old gods, no bloody-limbed girls. "I don't see how you can like it here," I say to Aurora. Her short hair suits her. She looks different, fiercer, somehow more herself.

"It's what you make of it." She reaches forward to touch the water. I cry out in protest, but she ignores me and drifts her fingers in the oily slick. As I watch, the darkness leaches out of it, dissipating like droplets of ink in a glass of water, until the river runs clear. I can see the pebbles in the riverbed. Tiny silver fish dart through the current. A frog regards me solemnly from the muddy bank before hopping into the water with a miniature splash. My nostrils fill with the rich scent of pine, the clean smell of warm earth, of high lonely places. Mountain smell. A marmot whistles. The sun is warm on my cheek. I raise my head. The black sky has gone blue; a lazy cloud drifts across it. The bone trees are sheathed in shaggy bark, branches sprouting green needles as I watch. Pine and hemlock, Doug fir. We're at the top of a pass. Around us, green hills rise to snowy ridges. I can see all the way to the edge of the world. The river burbles merrily on its long road to the sea, all its menace gone.

"You'll go back," she says. "You'll go back and you'll be so brilliant. You'll do all the things we said we would do. You'll be a famous painter. You'll travel. You'll see the whole world."

"I don't want any of that without you."

"You have to let us go."

I take her hand, match my twinned scar to hers. Palm to palm. She smiles at me.

"I don't know who I am without you, Aurora."

"You'll learn."

"I don't want to."

"You stubborn thing." She laces her fingers with mine and pulls me in. I hold her tight, so tight her breath catches. The smell of her skin, the flutter of her pulse against my cheek. "You were so brave," she says into my ear. "But I can't stay with you. You know that."

It takes all the strength I have to release her, but I do. I let go of her hand last. Jack quits his playing, sets the guitar aside, stretches. He kisses my cheek, and I lean against him for a moment. He stands, helps Aurora to her feet, picks up his guitar. She's wearing the same shirt she had on in the hospital. White silk against dark skin.

"I love you," I tell her, tell both of them. "I love you." I take off Cass's amulet and offer it to her. She closes my fingers around it, shakes her head.

"Stay frosty, babycakes. I love you, too." She touches my forehead, takes her hand away, looks at Jack. Walks away from me along the riverbank. After a pause, he follows.

"Aurora," I say. A jay calls behind me. The wind rustles through the trees. I know better than to expect either of them to turn around, but I can't help hoping all the same.

ACKNOWLEDGMENTS

I am deeply grateful to: My parents, for teaching me to trust my own voice; Justin Messina, peerless helper; Cristina Moracho, tireless draft-reader, jarmate, and boon companion; Emiko Goka-Dubose, for keeping me honest; Neesha Meminger, fellow revolutionary; Bryan Reedy, for bringing me here; Clyde Petersen, Carol Guess, Gigi Grinstand, Matt Runkle, Emily Barrows, Bojan Louis, and Meg Clark, support system extraordinaire; Cara Hoffman, Alexander Chee, and Madeline Miller, for kind words; Hal

Sedgwick, whose generosity sustained me; Elizabeth Hand, whose work continues to transform me; Michele Rubin and Brianne Johnson, the best agents in the history of the universe; Sara Goodman, for giving this story wings; Anna Gorovoy, whose design gave it a gorgeous home; Elsie Lyons, for the cover of my goth-girl dreams; the fabuloss publicist Jessica Preeg; Melanie Sanders, miracle among copyeditors; Lauren Hougen, for making it perfect; and last but not least, the Author-friends, especially Nathan Bransford, Tahereh Mafi, and Bryan Russell. Beloved cheerleaders, all of you.

This book would not have been possible without a fellowship from the MacDowell Colony.

READ ON FOR A SNEAK PEEK OF

DIRTY WINGS

COMING IN SPRING 2014 FROM ST. MARTIN'S GRIFFIN

NOW: BIG SUR

Before any of this, she thinks, there was the kind of promise a girl just couldn't keep. Before the bad decisions, before the night sky right now so big, so big it's big enough to swallow the both of them, before her hands shaking *stop shaking stop shaking stop shaking.* She is standing at the edge of a cliff, the edges of her vision sparking out into static, the heaving sea below her moving against the rocky shore with a roar. The wind is wild in her ears, singing her down. Not even the work of a jump. Just let yourself tip backward, let it go. Before any of this was there ever a chance for something different? The lowering moon swollen huge. Her hands ache, longing and more than longing. *If there were chords that said this.* Out there beyond the farthest reach of the world, out at the edge of everything, he is waiting for her. Bone-white face and long black coat and the knife-thin beckon of his mouth. His eyes darker than all the dark around her. The promise of him: honey flowing from the cracked earth, a crown of stars at her brow. The wildness of her despair at last made quiet. In her nostrils the heady tang of blood. A dog howls in the dark, three times. She can see the black palace on the white plain, its hundreds of doors open to welcome the night in. She takes a step forward.

"Hey, princess," says the familiar voice behind her. "Come on. Come back from there." Hand taking hers, pulling her away from the brink. "What are you doing? You're going to fall."

No, she thinks, *no, I want to go now,* but Cass's hand is insistent, bringing her back to her own skin, the solid earth under her bare feet. The madness leaching slowly out of the night. A car door slams somewhere behind her in the campground; a child shouts. "Maia. Come on. Girl. Come away from the edge." She shudders, thinks of leaping free like a deer, plunging into the abyss, and then the spell of Cass's gentle hands on her bare skin brings her back to herself and her twitching limbs still.

I'm coming, she thinks, *I will come,* even as she stumbles backward, clumsy feet carrying her away from the precipice. Back to the campfire's kind glow, their tent, Cass's arms around her, Cass's soft voice in her ear, murmuring,

"Come on, princess, one foot after the other, come on. Nice and slow."

I will wait for you, child, he says, his voice deep as stone in the heart of her. *I will wait.*

"I'll come," she whispers.

I know.

THEN

O scar is wearing his white suit today and he's unhappy with her. "Again," he says. "This passage. We will play only this passage, until it is correct."

He doesn't mean "we." He means her. His disappointment is like a rain cloud filling the room, drizzling resignation across his neat features and tiny frame. In the white suit he looks even more like a child: his ageless face unlined, though Maia knows he's at least fifty, his snowy hair still thick and unruly, his eyes bright and alert as an owl's. And as dispassionate.

"Do you see," he says, pointing to the page, in a tone that clearly indicates she does not. "Here is the song, here in the left hand. You bury it. We listen and we ask ourselves, 'Where is the story? Where is the beauty in this piece?' It is like listening to something that is very, how do you say? Muddy. You play this and it is a wall of mud, Maia." Oscar's English is perfect; he's lived in the States for decades. But he likes hamming it up when he's displeased.

"No mud," she repeats dutifully.

"The mud is very agonizing. I am saddened by the mud."

She nods. Sets her hands at the keys. Plays the arpeggios for him again, and again, and again, each time faster, each time more precise, as though by mastering the passage with near-inhuman speed she can somehow open up whatever it is that's closed in her. When she plays it for a tenth time, Oscar gestures to her to keep going and she surges forward, borne away by her own momentum, the notes rolling off her fingers, the music pounding through her and tumbling across the keys. When she's played through the étude Oscar straightens the lapels of the white suit and leans back in his chair.

"You are very good," he says after a long silence. "You know this. You are the most gifted student I have taught in many years. You work. You practice. You are serious. You have the ability to make a career. Even now, if we were not here"—he makes a sweeping gesture that encompasses the entirety of his house, the city, the backward corner of the world in which they have found each other—"if we were not here, and lived in a real place, a place of culture, who knows what would happen for you already. But you know what I am about to tell you. I say this to you always."

"No emotion."

"No emotion. Tell me, what is it you are so afraid of?" She is silent. "You will not tell me. This is unfortunate." His French accent thickens. "*Chérie*. You mustn't think as much as you think. You must breathe it. You must trust it with your own hands. This is why we practice and practice and practice, do you see, so that the notes become our own, so that we inhabit them until it is as though we wrote them ourselves. Until we see through to the other side. We are not *draft oxen*. It is not enough to *work*. Anyone can work. If you were only to work it would be better for you to shovel a ditch, do you see? For to only work, it is never to be great, and if you are never to be great there is no point in trying. You pick a profession that is sensible and have little babies and a house." He says "babies" with a tone of utter disgust. "This is all clear to you?"

"I want to be great," Maia says.

"I know this, I know you do. I see it in you. This fire burns. But it also destroys. If it is directed to the wrong place, it takes down your house. You look at me, here, all alone, I play for children. I do not mean you. For these wretched children with their runny noses, every day they come to me, their parents say 'Oscar, you make my child a musician,' and I say in my heart, 'I cannot make a peasant into the queen of France.' You must not end up like me. Broken and old. I could also have been great. I will never be great now. I am a sad man with a sad life, which I have ruined for myself, as you know. But you, child, your life is ahead of you."

"I'll try."

He purses his lips. "It is not a matter of *try.* Come, let us end on a pleasant note, if you will forgive me a little pun. Play for me Chopin's Sonata in B-flat Minor. The first movement, if you please. Do you know that Schumann said that this piece had something repulsive about it? It only goes to show you that there are Philistines in even the most unexpected places. But of course now we remember Schumann as a man who could have been one of the greatest composers of the nineteenth century if only he had been *coherent,* which is not a criticism we *apply* to Chopin, is it. 'Without melody and without joy,' Schumann said." Oscar sniffs. "*Incroyable.* Pollini has a very fine recording of the sonata, of course. Together we will listen to Federico Mompou, who is not a *fine* composer, but his Variations *sur un thème de* Chopin is quite amusing in some places, if rather vulgar."

"Huh," Maia says, and begins to play.

Oscar is placated by the Chopin and releases her at last. She gathers her things and he escorts her to the door, as he always does, though she's spent countless hours of her life in this house, knows the worn path from the piano to the front door so well she could mark it out with her eyes closed. Oscar's creaking old Victorian is nothing like her own beige-carpeted house with its white walls and spotless floors. Even now, the cleaning lady is probably bleaching counters, scrubbing toilets, washing already-clean white sheets. Oscar's house is an oasis of shabby majesty, littered with books and papers and dirty coffee cups, overflowing ashtrays teetering precariously atop stacks of newspapers and notebooks and sheet music. When she was little he'd let her linger after her lessons in his enormous library—an entire room full of nothing but books, crammed shelves stretching from the floor to the ceiling, books spilling over into piles on the floor. Books in French and English and Spanish and Italian, books about music and history and gardening and cooking. A disintegrating leather-bound set of the complete works of Balzac, translated into English, that she'd devoured in the drowsy afternoons until he sent her home to practice. Biographies of Ravel and Debussy and Chopin and Fauré, Rimbaud and Baudelaire, and Oscar's own teacher, Nadia Boulanger. A battered paperback of *Les Trois Mousquetaires* that she'd struggled through in the original French. If Oscar was very happy with her he would read passages aloud in a hilarious, affected baritone until she laughed so hard she cried.

Every room in Oscar's house is papered with ancient, hand-painted wallpaper, once grand but now peeling in long strips from the walls. His dusty wooden floors are scattered with threadbare Oriental carpets piled three or four deep; the windows are hung with velvet drapes, in some places so worn that light drifts through them to stain the dark floors gold. The disorder of Oscar's house is like a sanctuary. No one here to follow after her with a dustcloth, check the soles of her feet for dirt, demand she remake the bed until the spread lies without a single wrinkle, the ruffles falling from the decorative pillows just so. Not that Maia has friends who might see the dust ruffle askew. Oscar would catch a single wrong note out of a symphony, but Maia cannot imagine him so much as noticing if she moved a pile of dirt into his kitchen with a bulldozer.

Only Oscar's front room, the piano room, is tidy. Oscar

keeps his immense Hamburg Steinway—Maia has no idea how much it cost, or how he'd afforded it—polished to a spotless glow. No rugs on the swept floor, no shelves on the walls, no tables littered with teapots and packs of the Gauloises that his cousin sends him from Paris by the carton. No paintings, no chip-eared busts of famous composers, no highball glasses with a sticky smear of bourbon at their bottoms. Just the piano and Oscar's armchair, where he has sat and watched her play three times a week for the last fourteen years.

"Listen," he says now, one hand coming to rest lightly on her shoulder. "I wish for you to play something new."

"Okay." She stands the way her mother hates, one foot turned inward, resting her weight on its outside edge. He takes his hand away and disappears into the other room for a moment, returns with a sheaf of sheet music.

"What's this?" She riffles through the pages. "Ravel? I don't know these pieces."

"They are, how do you call." She resists the urge to roll her eyes. *"Difficile."*

"Comme tous les autres."

He laughs. *"Bien sûr, chérie.* We will begin with the first movement. *Ondine,* you will study. It must make you think of demons and that sort of thing."

"What?"

He clicks his tongue against his teeth. "Demons. Demons and ghosts. This piece, Ravel wrote for the night."

She keeps her face neutral, wonders if Oscar's finally shucked straight off his rocker. "Demons. Okay."

He beams, pats her shoulder. "Demons. Next week."

"Next week." As always, when he holds the front door open for her she has to fight the urge to curtsy.

It must have rained while she was at Oscar's; the sidewalks are slick and slug-streaked and there's still a faint mist to the world that leaves her cheeks dewy. If she walks home it'll take her an hour and there will probably be hell to pay, but she's restless for no reason, too antsy to wait for the bus that won't come for another twenty minutes at least anyway. She tucks Oscar's music into her shoulder bag. She can walk along the canal and cut over to the university before she reaches the freeway.

The January air has a chilly, damp edge to it, and she pulls her jacket tighter as she walks. The streets are empty. Her brown loafers make a neat tap on the wet pavement. She's tempted to step deliberately in a puddle, take some of the shine off the polished leather, but even tiny rebellions never go unnoticed in her house. Sit up straight, cross your legs like a lady, chew with your mouth closed, speak when spoken to. The severe line of her mother's unsmiling mouth, immaculately lipsticked in her immaculate white face. Tasteful pearl earrings, silk blouses without a single wrinkle, the delicate gold cross always at her throat. Blond hair pinned back into a neat chignon if she's teaching, spilling down her shoulders in rich honeyed waves if she's going out. The click of her heels—never in the house, never ever on the floors, no one wears shoes in the house. Her cool green eyes. When Maia was little her mother dressed her like a doll, ruffled pinafores and starched collars and a red wool coat that buttoned all the way to her throat; Maia still dreams about that coat sometimes, dreams where she's choking. Her mother dresses her still. It's easier than fighting, and anyway, what does she care about clothes. When she sees herself in a mirror, her dark hair sleek and straight, twins of her mother's pearl earrings—a sixteenth-birthday present from her father—dotting her own ears, pressed khakis, the loafers with their tassels falling neatly over her instep, she sometimes fails to recognize herself. And then she sees her brown face and remembers. Her skin makes it hard to forget.

She stops by the canal for longer than she should to watch a yacht make its stately way toward the Sound. Even this early in the year the water's dotted with kayakers, wetsuited against the chill. Their boats flash bright yellow and orange against the grey water, double-bladed paddles dipping with a rhythm like wings. Her father took her kayaking once, when she was very small. That was before he started drinking. They'd both been clumsy with the paddles, splashing more water than they moved through; Maia'd nearly upended herself in the lake. She remembers shrieking with delight, sun hot on her shoulders, the white sails of a nearby boat crisp against the blue sky. The water that close to her fingers, that far from shore, was disconcerting. If she'd fallen she could have tumbled endlessly through that deep green world to some alien kingdom at the bottom of the lake, where fish-finned women swam with their long hair streaming behind them like kelp. A palace she could almost picture, dark turrets rising against the darker depths. But there's no fear in the memory, only joy. The moments of her life when she was happy are easy for her to catalog because there are so few of them that aren't at a piano.

Unexpectedly, she's blinking back tears. "Stupid," she mutters to herself, scrubbing at her eyes with her fists. She turns away from the canal and keeps walking.

It takes less time than she thought it would to reach the Ave., and she wonders why she's never walked home from Oscar's before. If she hurries, she might even beat her mother home from her afternoon seminar. Her mother teaches the history of Ancient Greece; it's easy to impose order on dead civilizations. Maia's never sat in on one of her classes, but she can imagine the scene. Her mother, starkly beautiful, moving her elegant hands to illustrate the difference between kinds of spears. The front row of desks crowded with admirers. Students, eager to impress, writing down every word she says. Maia's seen the effect her mother has on other people, men and women alike.

Despite the chill in the air the Ave. is crowded. Students laden with books hurry to classes, a couple of dreadlocked hippies play Hacky Sack outside a coffee shop, a patch of scraggly street kids trailing hemp ropes and mangy dogs beg for change on a corner. Maia looks away from them, walks faster as she passes. One girl calls out to her. "Hey, princess. Spare a quarter?" Maia pulls her shoulders up to her ears. But the voice gets louder. "Hey, princess. Turn around. You got somewhere to be?"

Maia stops, turns. The girl's gotten up to follow her. She's about Maia's age, with wild-cropped blond hair dyed red at the ends. She's wearing a dog collar as a necklace, a filthy T-shirt under a cardigan three sizes too big for her, and a pair of camouflage pants tucked into black combat boots. But the most striking thing about her is her eyes—huge, grey pools Maia can't look away from. "You got somewhere to be?" the girl repeats. Maia shakes her head. Then, pan-icked, nods. "Which one is it?"

"Somewhere," Maia whispers. "Somewhere to be."

The girl looks her up and down. "Tea party? Etiquette lesson? Damn, girl, who put you in those shoes?"

"I don't have any money."

"Someone you know does." The girl's mouth twitches into a smile that's gone so fast Maia wonders if she imag-ined it. "Come on. Help me out."

"I really don't."

"Then help me out a different way. Look, I'm not from here. I need directions."

"Directions where?"

"Complicated directions. I need a map. Can you get me a map?"

"A map?" Maia repeats.

"You fashion-plated *and* deaf? Yeah, a map. They prob-ably got some kind of map in that convenience store. Of the area. Or the state. State parks. Like, any kind of map. But listen, you don't know me, right? So don't act like you know me. Because you don't. Come on."

"I told you I don't have money."

"Then get me a free one."

The girl propels Maia with one hand toward a conve-nience store across the street. Bemused, Maia lets herself be directed. Once they're inside, the girl whips her hand away and saunters over to the beer aisle, whistling. She pulls bottles out of the refrigerated case, puts them back again.

Maia looks for a rack of maps, doesn't see any. "Excuse me?" she says to the man at the register. He's watching the girl with a wary eye, doesn't notice her. "Excuse me?" she repeats, louder. He looks at her.

"Yeah?"

"Do you have, um, maps?"

"Maps of what?"

"Of, um, the area? Like a tourist map?"

Now he's irritated. "I look like a tourist to you, kid?" The girl is rummaging through bags of chips. "Hey!" he yells at her. "You ain't got money. I know you kids. Come on, get the hell out of here."

"No crime being in the aisle," she snaps back.

"It is if I say it is. Get."

She storms up to the cash register, knocking Maia aside with the full weight of her slight body. Maia can smell her skin. Sweat and, underneath it, something musky and wild. "I could call the cops on you," she hisses. "Fucking old perv."

The man at the register has gone from cranky to irate. "I mean it! Get the hell out of my store!"

She lifts her chin and widens her huge eyes. Despite the dirt, the ragged clothes, she looks like a queen. "I go where I want," she says softly, and then she turns and walks out the door. The man at the register scowls.

"Goddamn street kids," he mutters. "Someone oughta exterminate the lot of 'em. What kind of map you want, girlie? I got a street map."

"You have any free maps?"

"*Free* maps? Go to the goddamn *library*." He turns his back on her in disgust. For the first time it occurs to her to wonder why the girl didn't ask for her own map.

"Okay," she says. "Thanks anyway." He snorts.

Outside, the girl is waiting for her in an alley down the

block, one booted foot against a brick wall. She's smiling for real this time, a smile that's not going anywhere.

"I didn't get your map."

She puts both hands on her knees and hoots. Maia blinks, bewildered by her reaction. "I bet you didn't," she says, still laughing. "It's cool. Let me see your bag."

"No way," Maia says. "Look, I don't know what your deal is, but I'm going to go."

"Sure thing, princess. Just one minute, though." The girl pushes off with her foot and in one swift movement reaches into Maia's shoulder bag before she can protest. To Maia's utter astonishment, she pulls out two bottles of beer.

"Where did those come from?" Maia gasps.

"You stole them."

"I didn't steal anything!"

"What you think I was doing in there? Coloring? Come on, girl, don't tell me you're that dumb."

"I didn't—"

"You did. That deserves a drink, don't you think? Come on." The girl takes her hand, tugs her down the alley. Maia knows to say no. Maia knows to get the hell out of here, right now, get home, never come back to this corner again as long as she lives. The girl pries the bottles' caps off with a lighter and hands one to Maia. Part of Maia wants to take her hand again but she takes the beer instead.

The girl studies her. "I'm Cass," she says. "Short for Cassandra. The bitch who knew everything and no one would listen to."

"I know who Cassandra was. I'm Maia." She takes a sip, nearly spits it out. Beer foams over the lip of the bottle.

"You ever even drink before?" Maia shakes her head mutely, mortified.

"Well then. It's a day of firsts for you." That grin again.

"How did you even— I mean, I didn't even see you. You did it when you bumped into me?"

Cass rolls her eyes. "You live near here?"

"Yeah, up by the college."

"Fancy."

Maia shrugs. "My mom's a professor. My dad—" She stops. What is there to say about her dad? "My dad's a writer."

"Fancier and fancier."

"Where do you live?"

Cass laughs. "Where do you think, princess?" She points to a Dumpster. Maia's horrified.

"In *there*?"

Cass laughs harder. "Oh my *god*. Girl, where are you *from*? You're beyond real. Not in the actual Dumpster, no. I squat a place with some kids."

"Those people back there? With the dogs?"

"Some of them. People come and go."

"You said you weren't from here."

"I lied. You know how it is."

Maia has absolutely no idea how it is, cannot begin to imagine how it is. How does this girl eat? Take baths? What does she do for money? How did she get here? Does she have parents? Where does she sleep? Does she even have a bed? Maia considers which of these questions would be appropriate, decides none of them. "Do you like it?"

Cass shrugs, tilts her head back, finishes her beer. "Come on, princess, drink up. It'll do you good. We'll find some more and keep drinking."

Maia thinks, suddenly, about what time it must be, and her heart thumps wildly in her chest. "I can't," she says, handing her beer to Cass. "I have to go. Really. I can't. My mom—I can't." Cass looks at her again, that cool grey gaze.

"Maybe I'll see you again," she says.

Despite herself, Maia smiles. "Yeah," she says. "Sure."

6-27-14